THE LIGHT OF ETERNAL SPRING

ANGEL DI ZHANG

RANDOM HOUSE CANADA

PUBLISHED BY RANDOM HOUSE CANADA

 Published in 2023 by Random House Canada, a division of Penguin Random House Canada Limited, Toronto. Distributed in Canada by Penguin Random House Canada Limited, Toronto.

www.penguinrandomhouse.ca

Library and Archives Canada Cataloguing in Publication

Title: The light of eternal spring / Angel Di Zhang.
Names: Di Zhang, Angel, author.
Identifiers: Canadiana (print) 20220436266 | Canadiana (ebook) 20220436274 | ISBN 9781039004504 (softcover) | ISBN 9781039004511 (EPUB)
Classification: LCC PS8607.I2125 L54 2023 | DDC C813/.6—dc23

Text design: Jennifer Griffiths
Cover design: Jennifer Griffiths
Image credits: Skyler Dahan / Stocksy

Printed in Canada

10 9 8 7 6 5 4 3 2

Penguin
Random House
RANDOM HOUSE CANADA

For you

ONE

My mother died of a broken heart, or so the letter said.

I was standing before a vegetable stall in Manhattan's Chinatown, next to eight-for-a-dollar garlic and cabbage by the pound. The old Manchu woman who was translating spoke a broken, heavily accented English. She looked up from her lawn chair, and I stiffened under her gaze. I honestly didn't know how to feel. Death was an abstract thing for me; I had never been to a funeral.

I choked out the words. "What else does it say?"

"Just that your mother dead." The old woman thrust the letter back at me and circled two fingers in the air to ward off evil. She turned to a customer who was choosing peppers.

I glanced at the sun, directly overhead, the sky a painful blue unmarred by clouds, then down at the pavement at my translator's feet, as cracked as her heels in their torn embroidered sandals. Dazed, I lifted my camera from where it hung on a strap at my hip and took a photograph of her feet and the pavement laid with scars.

I fumbled with my purse and removed my wallet, almost dropping it on the ground. I offered her a ten-dollar bill for translating the letter even though she had volunteered to do it for free—a favor because she recognized a fellow Manchu in the shape of my face.

"No!" Her hand clamped on my wrist. "I give bad news. Go away. Your money no good."

I tried to think through the roaring in my mind. I understood her superstition, but also that she couldn't make much money selling vegetables on the street. "I want two heads."

Her eyes narrowed. "Chinese cabbage. Okay."

"And that." I pointed to the garlic. "Three dollars' worth. And that." I pointed again, to a bundle of spiky fuchsia fruits. All told, I bought Chinese cabbage I didn't know how to cook, twenty-four heads of garlic, and a pound of a fruit I couldn't name. It added up to twelve dollars and left me with two heavy bags to tote away. The white plastic stretched to translucence as I picked them up.

The absurdity of it all made me want to drop everything—the groceries, my purse, even my camera—and run through the streets.

Instead, I hobbled to the corner and hailed a cab, bent with a grief I could not process and food I could not eat.

I'D BEEN ON my lunch break, and headed back to the studio on autopilot. Outside the glass walls of my office, a single cloud in the shape of my mother's profile slipped across the sky, appearing first in one window, then the next. My eyelids felt heavy, but no tears came.

My purse had fallen open on my desk, the red lining highlighting the letter and FedEx envelope inside. I unfolded the paper along creases made by my sister's hands and touched the beautiful Manchu calligraphy, recognizing few words and understanding even less.

I dialed my sister's number in China, but it gave a fast busy and wouldn't connect. I tried several more times with the same result. Finally, I thought of my husband. His line rang four times before going to voicemail. "Hello, this is David Hilton of Prometheus Solar—"

I hung up.

"Come on, we're gonna be late." Martha, the art director, stood in the doorway. "Get the shot or else." She meant it as a joke, but her finger slid across her throat, lending edge to her words. My assistant, Joe, stood behind her.

I tucked the letter into my purse and closed it. I grabbed a scrunchie off my desk, braiding my hair while we walked to the studio. Martha's heels echoed down the hallway, her perfume of lilac and lavender weaving around me.

The rest of the crew waited in Studio One, where the ambient light seemed dimmer than usual. The model for this toothpaste ad was a six-year-old girl in flowered pajamas who sat patiently as the stylist fussed with her flyaway hairs and the makeup artist, seeking perfection, drew then erased the tip of one eyebrow. Another woman, presumably the girl's mother, hovered with a nervous smile.

I nodded, then walked to my workbench and picked a camera for the shoot. The metal weight of the Hasselblad medium format camera was reassuring, like holding my husband's hand. I dropped my head and peered down at the waist-level viewfinder, closed my eyes, and took a moment to breathe.

I need to tell someone my mother's dead.

Martha tapped my shoulder. "Enjoy your last time with that old thing. The digital cameras are about to arrive." She laughed when I frowned at her. The one thing that made sense to me in this moment—my camera—was about to make way for the future. Happy 1999.

I approached the model, who stood in front of a white sink before a window. It was lit from the other side to resemble a perfect sunny day.

I crouched to the girl's eye level. "Hello, my name is Amy. I'm going to photograph you today. What's your name?"

She shook my hand. Her grip was firm, the handshake of a prodigy. "Annabelle. Pleased to meet you."

"Okay, Annabelle, think of it as an afternoon play-acting with a friend. If you need a break at any point, tell me, okay?"

She nodded.

Joe loaded the camera with Polaroid film. He measured near Annabelle's face with a light meter, and I adjusted the angle of the studio lights. I took some Polaroids, then placed them on a table to develop.

After a minute, Joe scratched his head. "They're fuzzy."

"Hmm." Martha drew out the hum until it had shape and form.

I went to stand beside them. The six Polaroids were all out of focus—no edge where the sink met the window or where Annabelle's face met the light.

"Contrast is about right, and the lighting's good," Martha said. "Her cheeks have high color and her teeth look white. Check your focus." She glanced at her watch. "Oh my god, it's one thirty already. Just go ahead. Go with film."

I stared into the viewfinder. I thought the camera had been in focus.

I handed it to Joe, who loaded regular negative emulsion film. Then he and Martha fell back to join the stylist and makeup artist in the shadows.

I held my breath and refocused the lens on the girl. "You look great!"

Annabelle beamed, her mouth opening wide to display her teeth.

"Turn your head to catch the light, okay? A little more? Perfect! And again. Beautiful!"

After the first few shots, the rest of the world fell away as it always did when I was working. My past, my future, the nagging things that kept me awake at night. My mother.

Martha mimed instructions. "Okay, now open up the toothpaste, Annabelle. Do it slowly, so Amy can get the photos. Now put it on the toothbrush. You know how? You brush your own teeth at home?"

I rolled my eyes. The girl was six and already had a career. I'm sure she knew how to brush her teeth.

Two rolls of film later, Annabelle raised her hand. "Please, can I have a break? My mouth hurts from smiling."

I nodded and Annabelle's mother fetched her from the set, hugging her close.

Annabelle said, "Story time?"

Her mother nodded and led her to a bench in the makeup area, where they settled together. "Once upon a time, there was a goddess named Persephone," she said, and Annabelle suddenly looked exactly like a little girl.

My mother had told me stories when I was a child too, but hers never began with "once upon a time." Her stories took place at a specific location in a definite time. Like the story of Bo Le from the Gao kingdom, who in 650 BC recognized the quality of a horse that no one else could see.

"Was Persephone a princess?" Annabelle asked.

Annabelle's mother smiled. "No, she was a goddess. That's better than being a princess. The god of the Underworld kidnapped Persephone and brought her to his home beneath the earth. Her mother Demeter, who was the goddess of harvest and agriculture, searched for Persephone everywhere, forgetting to care for anything else, allowing the leaves to change color and fall off the trees, and the trees to sleep for winter."

My eyes unfocused. I pressed the heels of my palms into my closed eyes, pushing back the pressure in my head. I refused to cry in the middle of a photo shoot.

At the end of break, Annabelle's mother asked her, "Who's got a beautiful smile?"

"I do!"

"That's right, and you're going to share it with the whole world. Who loves ya, baby?"

"You do!"

I thought about how easy it was for Annabelle's mother to say "I love you," and how difficult it was for mine. Chinese girls are supposed to know their parents love them. Steeped in the ways of America, I wanted to be told. My mother had only said she loved me once, six years ago. On the last day we spoke.

THE APARTMENT WAS empty. I dropped my purse onto the dining table that already held books and teapots and vases and utility bills and set my camera beside it.

A Post-it Note on the fridge read "Compressor efficiency?" in David's neat handwriting. Inside the fridge was a pitcher of water, a half carton of eggs and many take-out sauce packets. I shoved the bags from Chinatown into it.

The light on the answering machine blinked red. I pressed play and David's voice filled the room. "Hi, darling. Alex needs the prototype for a demo tomorrow. It'll probably be an all-nighter. I love you." My fingers traced the cold, smooth edge of the answering machine. David's company was making more efficient solar panels by focusing sunlight. While we both captured light, I made art for myself and he made products to help the world.

I picked up the phone and dialed David's office. It went to voicemail again. This time I opened my mouth to say something, but nothing emerged. I hung up.

I dialed my sister in China. Between the country code, province code, city code and number, it was sixteen digits long. A ring right away, and then silence. I hung up and tried again. Perhaps I'd misdialed one of the numbers.

After an eternity of ringing, my father answered. "Hello?"

Disuse caused me to overemphasize the Mandarin Chinese words. "Hello, Father. It's me. Amy. I mean, Aimee . . ."

A thoughtful pause. And then a click.

I dialed again. Faint, distant clicks, as of insects crawling up the walls at night. Then the phone rang once, twice, three times; then four, five, six. It rang and rang, but no one picked up.

I hung up. He'd heard me. He must have. He hung up on purpose and didn't pick up again. He didn't want to talk to me.

I gripped the phone so tightly the seams on the plastic receiver incised my palm. Why had I said I was Amy? Aimee was the name my mother gave me.

I dialed once more and when no one picked up, I set the telephone receiver back in its cradle. Such a simple, complicated thing, this plastic device that could connect me to my family across the world. That should have connected me. After a moment, I picked up the phone and threw it against the wall. The receiver flew off and collided with a stack of books, the cradle clattering to the hardwood floor.

My mother was dead and I wasn't there. I wouldn't have the chance to set right everything that had gone wrong.

I kicked off my shoes, then gripped the lapels of my jacket and blouse and ripped, buttons ricocheting off books and chair legs and speakers and floor. I slid out of my pants and underwear and lay naked on the floor, my knees hugged to my heart.

TWO

Hours passed as the light outside my window changed. From the blue of late evening to the purple of night, overlaid by the weary orange of streetlights. I tried to conjure up memories of my mother. Of all the images and sounds, tastes and feelings that floated before me, the only thing I grasped was an idea—I had not known her well enough, did not love her enough, and now I never would.

I had never taken a photo of my mother.

In our living room there were paperbacks stacked two rows deep on bookshelves, newspapers piled on the coffee table, decorative cushions thrown on the couch and chairs and floor, artwork leaning against the bookshelves—so much stuff. So much everything.

When I was a child, I owned two sets of clothes for the summer and two for the winter. Success used to mean having enough food to eat, not a dozen hats that matched a dozen purses.

I usually found my stuff comforting, but not now.

My mother was dead and I had not been with her. I had been accumulating all these things.

I came to New York for art and stayed for love. Along the way, taking photos of girls and toothpaste, soup cans and candy bars, I lost track of the art.

On good days, I consoled myself that I was still working as a photographer, unlike friends from college who studied English literature but went into investment banking. On bad days, I wondered if I should have done something else for a living, something that would never compromise my photography. Doing the thing you love, but doing it wrong, ruins it.

This was also true of people. My imperfect love for my mother had ruined us.

I felt pinned to the ground by my books and clothes and furniture. Chilled and shivering, I eventually struggled to sit up and wrapped myself in a throw off the couch.

I groped through the stacks on the coffee table and found the photograph—not the one of New York that brought me to this country, but the one of David. In the photo, he is six years old, standing next to a swing set in his backyard in a Chicago suburb. His hands are cupped and lifted as he releases an adolescent pigeon, its wings blurred by motion. He'd nursed it back to health after finding it wounded. The kindness in his face always brought me comfort.

I hugged the photo to my chest. It was flat and offered no consolation. I stroked its edges with my fingertips, tried to lose myself in the image. The paper remained solid and sharp.

My limbs ached. I felt as if a new cavern of air had grown in the space between my heart and lungs.

ON THE DAY of my eighth birthday, my mother took me for a portrait. A traveling photographer had come to our village of Eternal Spring and set up in the main square where farmers gathered with their donkey carts to sell fresh produce.

As she prepared me to meet the photographer, my mother told me a story. "The Nishan shaman lived in the Ming dynasty—"

"From 1368 to 1644, before the Manchus defeated the Han and established the Qing dynasty," I interrupted, seated on a wooden bench, tapping the earthen floor of our living room with my birthday shoes.

My mother continued to braid my hair into two long plaits, one on either side of my head. "In her fiftieth year of life, a son was born to her." She winked, and I giggled. "She named him Sergudai—"

"What was her name? The Nishan shaman is a title, not a name."

My mother smiled and tapped the tip of my nose with her finger. "The Nishan shaman's name was Aimee." Like mine: *Ai* like the English pronoun "I," *mee* like the English "me."

I laughed, delighted. "When Sergudai was fifteen, he wanted to go on a hunting trip to Ice Dragon Mountain. His mother said that it would be dangerous, but Sergudai asked: 'Must a man remain in his home and never see the world?'"

"Can I go hunting to Ice Dragon Mountain when I'm fifteen?"

"No, you cannot, and don't ask me again. Aimee let Sergudai go, but he fell ill during the trip. When he got home, he died." My mother turned me on the bench and checked my braids. "The Nishan shaman was sad about her son's death."

"Of course she was!"

My mother retied the bows on my dress. I had tied them earlier, but I couldn't create the perfect bows my mother could.

"Aimee decided that she would solve the problem of her son's illness."

I tugged on my mother's elbow. "But her son was dead."

"He *is* dead."

"If he is dead, how can she fix his illness?"

"How are you normally?"

I giggled. "Cheeky?"

"No, physically."

"Healthy!"

"Right. If you were dead, would you still be healthy?"

I was sure something was being pulled over my eyes, but I didn't know what. "No?"

"Death is a kind of illness. As a cold robs you of the ability to breathe perfectly, and a flu robs you of the ability to breathe passably, death robs you of the ability to breathe at all."

I thought hard. "So if death is an illness, then . . . it can be cured?"

"Do you want to hear the story or not?"

"I do!"

She buffed the tops of my shoes with a cloth. "The Nishan shaman had her assistant prepare a hundred slips of paper as offerings. She put the crown of nine birds on her head."

"I thought only an empress wears a crown."

"Shamans do too. The nine birds perch on top."

"Why nine? What do they mean?"

"I don't know."

I blinked. There wasn't anything my mother didn't know. That's why she'd won the Teacher of the Year award two years running. There were things she didn't care about, yes, but not things she didn't know. "Really?"

"Eight is good, so nine is better."

"Eight is only good in Chinese because the word for eight, *ba*, sounds like the word *fa* for fortune. This is a Manchu story. Eight is not good or bad in Manchu."

My mother paused to consider my point. "Well then, I really don't know," she said and continued telling the story. "The Nishan shaman trembled like a weeping willow. She invoked, and the spirit entered her. She became dazed and fell down as her assistant sat next to her and beat a drum, chanting to guide her."

I listened with all my being. When my mother told magical stories, she also became magical.

My mother mimed, her unseen drumstick meeting her unseen drum. "Aimee walked through the Underworld, clutching the hundred slips of paper. Horse spirits galloped, crow spirits flew, and snake spirits slithered alongside her."

My mother checked my nails for signs of dirt.

"The Nishan shaman arrived at the banks of a river and saw a ferryman with half an oar and half a boat. One of the ferryman's eyes was blind." My mother went to poke my eye to demonstrate. I giggled and batted her hand away. "His nose was crooked"—my mother grasped my nose with her thumb and forefinger and twisted gently to one side—"and his ears torn." She reached out and tickled the tops of my ears. "His head bald, his legs lame and his hands twisted." I dodged as she tried to mess with my fresh braids.

"Aimee wrote her name on one of her hundred slips of paper and offered it to the ferryman. And because a name is a story, the ferryman accepted the paper and carried her across the river. And he was the one who told her the Lord of the Dead had decided to keep her son as his own.

"Aimee went to the City of the Dead. The gate was closed. The walls were high and solid. She summoned the hawk and the eagle and the vulture to fetch Sergudai and bring him to her in their talons.

"Sergudai was out playing when three giant birds seized him and flew over the walls of the city, setting him down in front of his mother. Aimee took his hand and they began their journey back to the Land of the Living."

My mother clasped my hand, and we left the house. The River of Stories, which ran by our yard, glimmered gold in the early morning light. We walked toward the village square. As we walked, my mother finished the story.

"The Lord of the Dead came out of the gates of his city and shouted, 'Shaman, wait! You cannot just take my son.'

"Aimee wrote words on three slips of paper and offered them to him, but he asked for more. She prepared another nine slips of paper, but again he asked for more. 'Write words on all the papers you have brought,' he said, 'and give them to me. In exchange, I will let Sergudai go.'

"'I will consider it,' the Nishan shaman said, 'if you will give Sergudai more years in the Land of the Living. It's not such a hardship for you, because after he dies, he will return here for eternity.'

"The Lord of the Dead nodded. 'I will give Sergudai twenty more years in the Land of the Living.'

"Aimee laughed. 'Why would I take him back if he will die before he can wipe his own nose?'

"'All right, I will make it thirty more years.'

"'Why take him at a time when his mind and heart are still undecided?'

"'I will add forty more years.'

"And so they negotiated until the Lord of the Dead had guaranteed her son ninety years of life. The Nishan shaman wrote words on all the remaining slips of paper and handed them over. Together, the words told the story of Aimee's rescue of Sergudai.

"On their way home, she had no slips of paper left to give the ferryman. So instead, she restored sight to his blind eye, and he carried them across the river.

"They passed the Ice Dragon Mountain, where Sergudai had fallen ill. They passed the banks of the River of Stories, where he had played as a child. And finally, they arrived home.

"The Nishan shaman's assistant helped her back into her body with his drumming, then awoke her with incense. She stood over Sergudai and fanned his soul back into his body. Sergudai sat up and said, 'I've had such fantastic dreams!'

"So, you see, the relationship between a mother and a child can bridge any distance."

I clapped for the end of the story, then said, "I had a year-long dream last night."

"What did you dream about?"

"I went to a world with Ainara and Yen where rabbits fly and dragons guard candy dishes. I had monkey friends and many adventures." My sister, Ainara, and our best friend, Yen, were often in my dreams, and I always believed they dreamed the same adventures I did—that this was how the world worked.

"How do you know your dream lasted a year?"

"I have memories from all four seasons. People made friends and got angry and had time to forgive and become friends again. In the dream, Grandfather Feng told me to draw a picture to prove to you where I'd been once I woke up, the way Father draws everything. But when I woke up, the drawing had disappeared." I swung my mother's hand and laughed. "Maybe if I took a photo in my dream, I could bring it with me when I wake up."

"Why would you think that?"

"I don't know, but there's something special about photography."

At the traveling photographer's studio, we climbed the steps of the covered wooden wagon. As my mother pulled open the door, a waft of air that smelled of vinegar and faded chrysanthemums escaped.

The studio was all one room and felt larger on the inside. A camera the size of a shoebox sat on its tripod in the center of the space. Its lens faced a fabric wall that rippled in the air currents created by our entrance. Scattered throughout the studio were fabric screens on wheels and metal lights on poles, a round table, a classic Chinese horseshoe chair, a pile of toys and a bicycle. A tall, slim woman stood in the middle of the space. Her hair was white, but her face had no wrinkles, so it was impossible to tell if she was young or old.

"This is Miss Zhang, the photographer who's going to take your picture," my mother said.

I stepped forward. "Hello. My name is Wu Aimee. The *Ai* is the *ai* of beautiful and the *mee* is the *mee* of potential."

"I'm so pleased to have you as my subject today."

I pointed to the black box. "Miss Photographer, how does the camera work?"

Miss Zhang placed a hand on the case. "I stand behind the body and point the lens at you, then cover myself with the cloth. When I pull the trigger, it takes your photo. What story do you want to tell, Aimee?"

"I don't understand."

"Every photo tells a story. Some people even say that a photo is worth a thousand words."

"That's silly. How can they know one photograph isn't worth five hundred, while another, one thousand and twenty-one?"

Miss Zhang laughed. "A story begins with a character." She pointed at me. "Then it adds a background, something for the character to interact with." She gestured to the rippling wall strung with painted backgrounds on rods. "You're going to be the character, so now you need to choose a background."

I stood back while she unrolled options in front of me: a desert, a forest, a traditional sitting room with rosewood furniture, a zoo. My mother preferred the sitting room but said I could choose. I chose the lake bordered by a weeping willow. Perhaps there was such a lake in the town that was an hour away by horse-drawn cart. If not there, then certainly in the city of Harbin, where my aunt lived. That was the setting I wanted.

I stood in front of the background and posed, one hand on my hip.

My mother stood assessing me, her right foot turned out, one hip higher than the other. "Wait a moment." She turned me by my shoulders and smoothed the already glassy surface of my hair. She tugged at my dress to make sure that the hem was perfectly straight, then rubbed away an imagined spot of dirt on my chin with her thumb.

I posed again, this time with both hands on my hips.

"Sorry, wait a moment," my mother said. "She doesn't look natural, does she? You're posing stiffly, Aimee, like you're having your photo taken."

"But I *am* having my photo taken."

The photographer smiled. "A lot of children pose that way."

My mother pursed her lips and walked in a slow arc around me. She accidentally kicked the bicycle and reached out to steady it. Then she lifted it and brought it to me. "Ride the bicycle. That looks like something you might do every day."

"But I've never been on a bicycle."

"Come on, it's easy."

The photographer steadied the bicycle as my mother helped me on. I gripped the handlebars, clenched my teeth and smiled, my bottom an inch above the seat, both feet planted on the ground.

My mother beamed. "Good. You look perfect."

Through gritted teeth, I said, "I'm riding a bicycle in a lake!"

"Good?" The photographer smiled at my mother, and when she nodded, ducked under the black cloth at the back of her camera. "Don't blink."

Poof!

For a moment, the room was ablaze with light, and all I could think of was blinking.

Miss Zhang reappeared, smiling. "I will have the photo printed by tomorrow. You can get off the bike now."

While my mother spoke with her about the number of prints she wanted, I wandered to a round table. Light fell on one half, rendering it a gibbous moon. In the center of the table was a black photo album, the size of an adult hand.

I opened its cover.

❦

THE PHOTO I stared at was unlike any I'd ever seen: a grainy black and white cityscape from the vantage point of a roof. Light fell on both sides of the buildings. The sky that should have been clear or cloudy was instead riddled with dotted lines resembling Morse code. The buildings were too tall, reminding me of the unbuilt wonders in my father's sketchbook. He was an architect, but our village was home to only 900 people and his designs were too grand.

My heart beat so fast I grew dizzy. The photograph focused and then unfocused before me, and I gripped the edges of the table for balance.

A spotlight illuminated me in a perfect circle.

Snow fell from a ceiling that stretched higher and higher. I opened my mouth and laughed as snowflakes gathered on my tongue. They tasted of that flavor that is particular to the first snow of winter.

I looked around and the photographer was gone, as were the backgrounds, props and my mother. Snowflakes landed on my open palm—no, not snow but round dandelion heads, one of which exploded with a pop, releasing fluff into the air.

I look down at the photograph again.

I fall in.

I emerge standing on the pavement of a street limned with light, gazing up at buildings taller than any I have ever seen. The air smells metallic: the iron of humanity, not the dirt of earth. Car horns blare and people talk in a language filled with harsh consonants. In the back of my mouth, I taste the sweet, herby flavor of dandelion pollen.

Since I don't know where I am, I don't know who I am, and the thought thrills me.

Tenderly, I touch the closest wall. The gray concrete surface feels stronger than any mud-brick wall in Eternal Spring.

"Come on, Aimee," I hear my mother say.

I fall out.

I still stood in a shaft of light, but the edges where light met darkness softened. The smell of iron faded into vinegar and chrysanthemums. My mother pulled my hand to leave.

"Wait! That photo, where is it?"

The photographer said, "Niu Yue." New York. *Niu* was the Chinese for twisted, and *yue* sounded like the Chinese for moon. Twisted Moon.

I imagined the perfect circle of a full moon, rotating and flipping over on itself. I imagined a moon that could light a place eternally.

I didn't know if New York was a street or a city or a country, only that I wanted to be there. I wanted to be where everything was bright and tall and three-dimensional, where light shone on both sides of the buildings and there were no shadows. And I wanted to become a photographer so that I could capture the light.

I thought of Sergudai's words when he turned fifteen: "Must a man remain home forever and never see the world?" I decided that I wanted to go to Niu Yue, even if the cost was death. At eight, I didn't understand that it might not be *my* death.

WHEN WE GOT home, I went next door to my friend Yen's house, not to find Yen but to see his grandfather. Feng sat at the dining table, contemplating a sheet of blank paper.

"Hello, Grandfather Feng."

"Cricket, ladybug." He didn't look up.

I sat and leaned my arms on the tabletop, lacing my fingers. "I have a story to tell you. It's a story about a girl. Not me. The girl is also smart and pretty and has good grades."

Feng grunted and tried to stand the sheet of paper on its edge. Unsuccessfully.

"This girl, she isn't a shaman, but she has the magic to travel into photographs. One day, she falls into a photo of a faraway land. In the photograph world, there are tall buildings, a sky of ever-changing secrets, and people who hurry past her so fast she can't focus on them."

Bang! Feng slapped the sheet of paper down and pinned me with an intent stare. "You fell into a photo."

"It's a story, Grandfather Feng."

He laughed. "All your stories are about you. Even when it's not about you, it is about you. And especially when it's about you, it's about you."

I nodded. "Yes, you're right. Mother took me to a photographer's studio today. While I was there, I fell into a photo." I leaned forward, waiting for a response. Feng sat still. "The photographer told me it was of a place called Niu Yue. It was amazing. The buildings were so tall and the sounds so loud. When I grow up, I'm going to go there."

Feng's eyes narrowed. "I can't help you go. Why are you telling me this?"

"I have to tell someone, otherwise I might burst." I pulled on my forearm, checking for the seams that might unravel.

"And telling me doesn't matter because if I repeated it no one would believe me. Because I'm crazy." Feng threw back his head. His laugh was clear and unfiltered, an honest child's laugh. "Are you afraid you're crazy, Aimee? You're not crazy."

I breathed better.

"Not any crazier than I am anyway."

I breathed worse.

Something in his expression shifted. "What you are is magic. You can fall into photos, which means you can travel where others cannot. In another time, you might have been a shaman."

Shamans lived in stories. It sounded crazy for Grandfather Feng to call me a shaman, so I kept it a secret and never told anyone else in Eternal Spring that I could fall into photos.

THREE

Dawn light slanted through the windows, highlighting the telephone strewn across the floor. I placed the receiver back in its cradle, then dialed my sister again several times. I got a fast busy signal and silence. I hung up.

I picked up my camera from where it rested on the dining table. My secondhand Nikon had been a constant companion since my junior year at Columbia University. I'd worked at the library to afford it, shelving books at a rate of 100 an hour for 115 hours. My camera came at the cost of 11,500 books shelved: many thousands of words.

I dressed in David's old football jersey and grabbed rolls of film from my purse.

My closet darkroom was a tiny room lit sometimes by an incandescent light and other times by a bare red bulb. The air blossomed metallic at the back of my throat. It was just large enough to fit a narrow table, a photo enlarger and me. Overhead, prints dried in the air on a cat's cradle made of metal clips and twine.

I placed my camera and film cartridges on the table, among trays, chemicals, tongs and photo paper.

Pinned to the wall above were the photos I loved most: the one of New York City that brought me here, the one of Yellowstone National Park in moonlight, the one of David as a child with his pigeon.

I closed the door and turned out the incandescent light, which David had rigged to simultaneously turn on the do-not-disturb sign outside the door.

From Polaroids, I had learned the length of a minute. In complete darkness, while I developed film, time dilated to the air entering and exiting my body. In the printed photo, time had the grace to pause. I closed my eyes, not because it would be darker with them closed, but because rhythm changes when I don't have to blink. Closing my eyes made the darkness my choice.

My fingers felt for the controls on the back of my camera and clicked to rewind. When I opened the latch, the cartridge leaped into my hand. I unrolled and dipped and dunked and breathed intoxicating chemicals as the film developed.

I turned on the red safelight and opened my eyes. My world blazed, going from complete darkness to a single red light. The contrast of everything was so stark, and even the blackest black of a shadow was tinted red.

The first photo was a sharply delineated tree at sunrise. The light bursting from behind the trunk made the entire tree seem aflame. With the print squarely on the table in front of me, I placed one hand on either side, dropped my head and leaned in hard.

The tree morphed into blobs of reddish-gray ink splatters on paper, but then coalesced into branches and leaves. The wood of the tabletop pressed back against my palms, too solid. I counted several heartbeats. Nothing happened. I smacked the table.

Every day, I began my mornings in darkness, developing the photos I'd taken the day before. Eagerly I hoped, wished, prayed for the one I could fall into. The one that would make all the others—that would make me—make sense.

Every day, I failed.

On happy days, the failure spurred me to go out and take more and better photos. To try new film, lighting techniques, subjects.

That day, it was just failure.

I turned on the incandescent light. Warm, orange-tinted.

The next photo was the one of the Manchu woman in Chinatown who had translated my letter. The photo was so blurry that the cracks in the pavement and on her heels were not there, as if the photo had been taken through a window during a spring downpour. I touched the print.

I had never taken a photo so out of focus.

I reviewed the thirty-six thumbnails on my contact sheet. The first few were perfectly sharp. Then came the news of my mother's death, and everything within the following frames was blurry.

I frowned and set down the contact sheet. I opened my camera body to inspect it, but the interior was pristine. I unscrewed the lens, peered through it from one end and then the other, checked for scratches or smudges that could scatter light in the wrong direction. Nothing.

A tumbling click-click came from the front entrance, then heavy footsteps. The door of my darkroom opened behind me. I smelled cinnamon and coffee.

The daylight that for a moment illuminated my darkroom was filtered by hands cupped over my eyes.

"Guess who?" David kissed my ear.

"I know who," I said, as I pulled his hands from my eyes.

"I have good news," he said.

I turned to face him and he lost his smile.

"Amy, what's wrong?"

Seeing myself reflected in his eyes, the tears I'd tried so hard to shed the night before finally came. "I got a FedEx letter from Ainara. I took it to get translated at lunch yesterday. My mother's dead."

He hugged me hard.

"She died of a broken heart. And it's my fault."

David stroked my hair. "How could you possibly think that?"

I pushed him to arm's length. "A *broken heart*, David!"

He pulled me in again.

"I should have known when she died. How could I not have known?"

"She lives on the other side of the world—"

"I should have known."

David tried to lead me from the darkroom, but my feet were rooted to the spot.

"All right," he said. "First you need some coffee." And like a magician, he disappeared, only to return with a cup of coffee from my favorite shop. "Here."

I cradled the cup in my palms, felt the heat seep into

my fingers. I closed my eyes and took a sip, swallowed, took another sip.

David waited for me to drink half the cup, then he said, "When's the funeral?"

"It might have already happened. Ainara only wrote that our mother was dead. Or maybe she didn't tell me about the funeral because she doesn't want me there."

"Call her."

"I did. My father answered and hung up on me."

"He what?"

"The connection to the village is always bad, but I heard him say hello. Then he hung up. I called back and no one answered. And when I tried again, it wouldn't connect."

"What do you want to do?"

"I don't know! I'm just so angry that my mother and I . . . that it's been so many years since the last time I saw her. I didn't realize how much I had to say to her."

I put my empty coffee cup on the darkroom table. In David's eyes, I saw sympathy but not understanding. "I can't hear her voice. Do you remember it?"

"You know she never spoke to me."

"Who doesn't remember their mother's voice?"

David drew me back into his arms, saying, "Yes, the two of you stopped talking. But I'm sure she knew you loved her. Even without words."

I shook my head. "When I told her I loved her, she laughed. And she only said it once to me. We were fighting and I goaded her into it."

My alarm clock beeped.

Feeling guilty about many things, I walked to the bedroom and turned it off. "I have to leave for work in half an hour."

David caught me by the arm. "No, you don't. Call in and tell them you need time off. The quicker you get home, the better your chances of making the funeral."

"I can't just walk away. I have a lot of projects to finish."

"Your mother died." David kissed my free hand. "They'll understand."

It hadn't even occurred to me to go to China. I hoped it was out of shock but suspected it was fear. Fear of how I would be received. If I would be received at all.

"With the time difference, it's one whole day just to get to Beijing," I said, "and then another to Harbin. And then to Eternal Spring. Two or three days each way to go and come back. Plus the time there. So I need more than a few days."

"It'll be all right. You've been working at the agency for six years and never taken more than a long weekend."

"Okay." I nodded.

He opened the dresser and handed me his passport. "Take mine with you and get us both visas."

I frowned. "You're coming with me?" David and his friend Alex had taken their graduate engineering thesis and founded a company to make solar panels. They were going to convert us all from burning oil to capturing light. I wasn't the only one who never took a day off.

"Of course, I'm coming with you. You couldn't be there when she died but maybe we'll make it for the funeral."

People worked six days a week in China, so Sunday would be the most logical day to hold a funeral. If I hurried, maybe there was still a chance to say goodbye.

❀

FROM MY FIRST memory to my fifteenth birthday, I lived in the village of Eternal Spring at the tri-border junction of China, Siberia and North Korea. Three hundred and fifty years before I was born, the Manchu tribes united and conquered China. The Chinese people outnumbered the Manchu, so over time the culture of the conquered enveloped the conquerors. By the time of my childhood, we were all Chinese.

Our house was built of straw brick, two rooms shared by my mother, father, my maternal grandmother, my little sister, Ainara, and me. Ice Dragon Mountain guarded us from the north and the River of Stories ran near the western wall. The government was rationing food, so in the yard, we raised a few ducks and chickens, two pigs and rabbits.

The door opened into the kitchen, and the kitchen into the living room. It was a real living room in the sense that we did all our living in it: ate, studied, entertained and slept. A molded mud-brick platform ran through the interior wall. On the kitchen side, it was the base of a stove topped by a giant wok; on the living room side, it was the *kang*, a communal bed where we all slept, side by side. The fire that cooked our meals became the embers that heated our bed.

Our cat lusted after two fish that swam in a bowl on top of the dining table, our dog tormented the cat, my father chased after the dog to make sure he didn't hurt the cat, and my mother chased after my father to make sure he didn't hurt the dog. It amazes me to this day that given all the times I saw the cat pawing the open lip of the bowl, I don't remember losing a fish.

When it rained, my architect father would climb onto the roof using a wooden ladder and repair the areas where water leaked. After drying off, he would draw plans for buildings made of iron and cement—materials we didn't have. I understood that art was permanent where all other things were temporary, and I wanted to be an artist like him.

One day, my father recycled two industrial fluorescent light tubes by scrubbing out the milky interior coating. He filled them with water and some baby electric eels he'd caught in the river. He stood the tubes in the far corner of the living room. At night, after we all lay down to sleep, the cat would sit mesmerized in front of the slithering eels, their bodies lit from within. The eels were our only electricity.

Every autumn, winds from the Eastern Sea blew iodine across the water to Eternal Spring. The iodine seeped into us and inspired new ideas. One autumn afternoon, my aunt Eyun, who was my mom's sister, came home from Harbin city for the Moon Festival. She told me love was the most confusing thing in the world.

Eyun was born with black hair the same as every Manchu girl, but after she left Eternal Spring to study, then work, in the city of Harbin, her hair turned red, the color of fire just ignited.

We both knew Manchu, but we talked in Chinese because that was the language the world spoke.

"I met a man." She blushed, a pink that suffused her cheekbones and spilled to her ears. "He is from Xinjiang province, and he works with me at the factory."

"And?"

"And he is nice. He is smart. Top of his provincial exams at university."

"Like you." I sat on the stoop of the house, sure I would be there for a while. Eyun told her stories slower than my mother did, measuring her words like a scientist. She only visited for holidays, but I felt closer to her than to my mother's brothers, who lived on the other side of the village. Eyun sat next to me.

She watched the light dancing on the surface of the River of Stories. "He is an engineer. Skilled at fitting things together so they become aerodynamic and—"

"What's aerodynamic?"

"What do they teach you in school?"

"I'm eight years old! One day I will leave home like you and learn everything in the world, but I'm not there yet."

Eyun laughed. "Aerodynamic is when wind blows over something as if it were not there." A ladybug landed on the back of Eyun's hand, and she held it up. "See how round and smooth the ladybug's body is? This is aerodynamic."

"So he makes planes?"

"Something like that."

Her gaze drifted, and I prompted her back. "He's not ugly or anything?"

"He's handsome! His hair is curly at the ends, long enough that it brushes the top of his collar when he turns his head—"

"Have you told him how you feel?"

She shook her head. "He should tell me first."

I frowned. "What if he's waiting for you to go first?"

"That's silly. He should know. He's smart. He'll figure it out."

"Mm."

"Who'll figure what out?" my mother asked from behind us.

I opened my mouth to speak but closed it again, making the air-kissing sound of a hungry fish.

"Nothing important." Eyun raised one eyebrow at me, then stood to enter the house.

As I got up to follow, my mother grabbed me by the wrist. "Come help me get carrots."

Having no good excuse to escape, I followed her to the root cellar hut in the yard. It was built with solid chunks of local rocks, mud and straw, and served as a fridge. The door was, in a previous life, the door to some other room. Slivers of blue paint peeked out among gray splinters. The sides of the hut were banked with earth three feet deep for insulation. My mother used a shovel to dig out the door and opened it just wide enough for us to slip in.

My first breath always caught me by surprise; the scent of clay floor, potatoes, rice, garlic, salt and spices combined to produce something earthy and delicious that made me salivate every time. My skin tingled in the chill.

"Tell me about this man."

"He—wait, what man?"

"My younger sister's man."

I toyed with a strand of my hair. "There's no man."

My mother narrowed her eyes. Had the light been bright enough, she might have looked menacing. But her voice was the melody I had grown up with, of which I could never be afraid.

"No man here," I said. "Really." This was true, as my father was out putting up the lights that ran through the village for the Moon Festival. "And Eyun, if she has a man, which I'm not saying she does, but if she did have one, I would not tell you about him. And if she didn't have one, I still wouldn't tell you because then you'd worry she's already twenty-five and not yet married."

"I do worry." My mother dug into a box of sand for the carrots buried there. A scar shaped like four branching lines of lightning flexed on her wrist. "You are too young to understand, but there is an order to the world. A way that things and people are supposed to be. Laoyue, the old man of the moon, ties the red ribbon of fate. On one end is you, on the other is your *dui xiang*." Soul mate.

She paused. Her next words came slower and felt less ruled by gravity, as if they might float from our hut, down the street and beyond the village. "Sometimes I wonder if Eyun herself understands. Marriage isn't just about the man and the woman, but also about the man's family and the woman's family."

Confused by this change in her, I beamed a smile. A ladybug flew through the slice of light left by the door and landed on my forehead, its legs tickling me.

My mother placed her finger in the ladybug's path, and it climbed on. "It's good luck when a ladybug lands on you. Each of their dots tells the story of a dream, or a journey or a loss."

"How do you read them?"

"They surround you." She pointed, and a dot on the ladybug's back glowed with light. When that dot faded to black, a different dot lit up. Soon the dots flashed like a dozen fireflies dancing on a warm summer night. The first dot flashed three times and stayed lit. Dust motes haloed my mother as she sang to the ladybug in Manchu. It raised its red shell to reveal lacy wings and flew away.

"So, Eyun—"

"I can't be bribed with stories."

My mother pursed her lips. A shadow blocked the door.

"Hello, hello," the shadow called. It was Yen, our best friend. He was two years older than me, and three years older than Ainara. He dreamed of becoming an astronaut and touching the light of the stars. China didn't have a space program, and the adults thought his dreams too grand, but I thought that's what dreams are meant to be.

"Hello, Yen!" I waved my hand through the gap in the door.

My mother handed me the enamel bowl of carrots and I carried it out into the light, grinning at my friend.

Yen held a shovel in his hand, which he used to help my mother rebury the hut after she'd shouldered the door shut. After the last shovelful, he announced, "My older brother got accepted at Jilin University. It's a great day for our family. We've never had a university student before."

My mother said, "Congratulations to your family! That's wonderful news."

"Congratulations!" I echoed.

Yen nodded happily. "Thank you. We are all proud, my mom and dad and me. Of course, Mom might be too excited."

My mother frowned. "What do you mean, too excited?"

"Mom has been hoping so hard that her vision got funny. We thought it would clear up once we got the good news, but it hasn't. Grandpa Feng says people can go blind from emotion and that when she's ready, she will see again. But she has a white film over her eyes."

My mother led the way back to our house where they put away the shovel. "You mean an infection or a fungus?" she asked.

"I don't know, but it isn't right. I thought I could ask Dr. Sun what she thinks, and if she has some medicine for it." Dr. Sun was my grandmother, a doctor of Traditional Chinese Medicine.

My mother made sympathetic clucking noises. "She's not here. She's taking care of a man with bronchitis across the village." She studied his downcast face, then went to the medicine cabinet. "Let me see if I can find something."

The cabinet was made of rosewood and its lid opened to form a table. Inside were many little drawers, each with a carved half-moon handle. My mother squinted and pulled out one drawer after another. Finally, she plucked a half-used tube from one of them. "Ah, here it is. It will clear your mom's vision. Apply a bit to her eyeball twice a day."

"Thank you so much."

As Yen bolted for the door, we waved.

"Don't be a stranger," my mother called, then rounded on me. "Now about your Aunt Eyun—"

I giggled and ran as she laughed and chased me.

MY MOTHER FORGOT to tell my grandmother about Yen's visit. A week passed. I was sitting at the dining table doing homework under my grandmother's gaze when Yen returned, all smiles. "It worked! It worked! Thank you, thank you."

Odd, how people say things twice when they're happy, as if we didn't hear them the first time. I kept at my homework, adding columns of numbers, drawing equal signs with a ruler.

My grandmother lowered her newspaper. "What worked?"

"Aimee's mother gave me medicine for my mom's eyes, and now she can see clearly again."

My grandmother smiled. "I'm glad."

"I've come to return the rest of the medicine in case someone else needs it in the future." Yen handed the tube to my grandmother, who set it on the table.

After he'd gone, she frowned at the tube, picked it up and stared at it. She shook her head and muttered something. I looked up. She gestured for me to return to my homework.

When my mother got home from the market, my grandmother said, "Yen came to return the eye medicine."

"It didn't work?" my mother asked.

My grandmother raised one eyebrow. "It worked. Except . . ."

"Except what?"

"Except it's not eye medicine." She held out the nearly empty tube. "Read it."

My mother took it and brought it close to her face, then held it far away, then close again. "Miracle Athlete's Foot Medication—it fixed her eyes though, huh? Well. That's good." She shrugged with an embarrassed smile.

"What about *your* eyes? Did you pass the eye exam this year?"

"I'm the teacher of the year. The eye chart hangs on the back of my door every day except when the nurse uses it to test the kids and teachers." My mother enunciated each shape with slow precision. "The character is open to the east, open to the west, open to the south, open to the east—"

I laughed until I almost fell off my chair. "You memorized the eye exam chart!"

She put a finger against her lips to shush me. "You can't go around spreading that story."

"Why not? It's a great story. Also, you told me never to lie."

My grandmother laughed.

I regarded my shamefaced mother. "You must march right over to Yen's house, young lady, and tell them the truth."

My mother pointed at me. "Not funny."

"Why is it okay to lie to Yen?"

My mother sat and pulled me into her lap. Her dress smelled of fall leaves. "Let me tell you a story. When your aunt Eyun was a child, she learned how to sing happy birthday to our grandmother in Manchu. She practiced every day for a week. But when the big day came, she sang the words wrong. Grandmother was already deaf, so she just clapped along happily. We never told her, because it wouldn't help her to know Eyun had made a mistake, and Grandmother was happy thinking that she'd learned the song perfectly in her honor. Sometimes a lie hurts no one, and actually protects people."

I chewed on my lower lip. "What you're saying is, if you have to tell a lie to accomplish something good, then it's good to tell a lie?"

My mother nodded.

"So I won't tell Yen, but I'll tell the school nurse so she can get you a pair of glasses?"

My mother tucked a length of stray hair behind my ear. "It would be good of you to say nothing at all. I will go to the nurse and get the glasses myself."

I held out a curled pinky finger. My mother hooked her own in mine. We both pulled, sealing the pact.

As I floated toward sleep that night, my eyes filled with the light of the Milky Way outside our single window, my mother whispered in my ear. "So, this man of Eyun's . . ."

"I'm asleep, Mother."

I'M GLAD I hadn't told my mother about Aunt Eyun's man. By the time my aunt came for Chinese New Year, five months later, everything had changed.

I loved Chinese New Year. It was a time of endings, but also of beginnings. It held so much possibility, so many things to be experienced by the new-year me that the old-year me hadn't been able to imagine.

At sunrise, the River of Stories froze into a mirror that reflected a crystalline image of Ice Dragon Mountain. A storm arose. The blinding white made me forget that there was a world outside our house, outside my family.

I marveled that our dining table could survive the assault of a dozen plates stacked, one overlapping the next, each piled high with delicious and rare holiday food. Each New Year's also brought two new sets of clothes that my mother had managed to sew in secret, so as to surprise us when the time came. And the best part was that all our relatives, near and far, would come to visit. My uncles brought their families from the other side of the village. My Aunt Eyun came home from the city. And this year she brought a guest, the handsome young man, whose name was Jian.

My mother chopped onions in the kitchen, having swallowed a mouthful of salt water so they wouldn't make her cry. "So Auntie Eyun's man that does not exist is from the south."

My fingers stilled on a half-peeled garlic clove. "I thought he was from the west?"

"South or west or east. If it's in China, it's all south of here."

My father heard her as he came in the door. Snow swirled around him, grasping at his calves and ankles. "That is not true. There must be . . . what? Three or four houses north of here, but south of Siberia."

My mother smiled and wiped her hands on her patchwork apron. It had originally been my shirt and my sister's pants, both given new life after we wore out the elbows and knees, respectively. "And did you find any fish between here and Siberia? Or should I have sent someone younger?"

He laughed heartily. "Do I have a fish? Jian, come in."

Jian entered the house, holding up a fish. My mother and I gasped. The fish weighed maybe a pound.

"That's enough fish for me," I said. "What about everyone else?"

My mother raised an eyebrow at them, but both men guffawed, and the candlelight in the room brightened. "That is the first fish we caught." My father brought out the arm he'd held behind his back. "But this is the fish we're going to eat tonight."

Jian needed both hands to hold on to the new fish my father passed to him. The tail curled on the ground, still writhing.

I ran to the fish and looked up at my father. "The fish is bigger than me!"

"And heavier too. It's a good thing Jian went fishing with me this holiday."

"Thank you all for inviting me. It's very generous of you to have me on New Year."

Jian is handsome, I thought, but maybe a little too pleasant.

Aunt Eyun came to the doorway from the living room. She blushed again, as she had when she first spoke to me of Jian.

My mother waved them away. "Go, warm up and wait for food. I'll make fish stew. Lots and lots of fish stew." In Chinese, *yu* is the word for fish and sounds like the word *yu,* for surplus. To have lots of fish is to have abundance.

My father and Jian lifted the fish onto the counter and then followed Aunt Eyun into the living room to tell tales of their expedition.

My mother patted the fish on the head and fetched a giant rolling pin from a high shelf. She tipped her head thoughtfully left then right, one hand behind the fish's gills. "This is the best way to kill a fish. You knock him, and he forgets himself."

"Forgets himself?"

"Forgets he is a fish. Or he is at all."

I came closer to watch.

"You have to hold on to the gills, so he doesn't slide around." She slipped her thumb and index finger into the fish's head. She raised the rolling pin high in the air and brought it down on the bridge of the fish's nose with one decisive whack. The wriggling stopped immediately.

My mother traded rolling pin for cleaver and cleanly severed the head. She turned the body upside down and found a tiny hole in the belly of the fish with the tip of her sewing scissors. With one gliding stroke of her arm, the fish lay open, tightly packed organs spilling out onto the counter. She placed them into a bowl and set them aside.

She scaled the fish by sliding the top of her cleaver from tail to neck. Silver scales exploded into the air. "You have to make them forget this life or they don't go into the next life so easily. When I was a girl, I saw the mother of a friend cooking fish. She didn't know about knocking it out. She just cut the head off. The poor fish opened his mouth and tried to talk but no words came out. He tried to talk for almost an hour, eyes bright, watching his own body being deep-fried and topped with garlic."

"But how can a fish talk with only a head?"

"Their brains and their hearts are all in their head, right next to each other. Fish are honest—they have to tell you what their hearts feel."

My mother sliced the fish and placed a large portion of flesh in the wok, then added garlic, ginger, soy sauce and vinegar. She covered the wok with a wooden lid and wiped her hands on a towel. She whispered, "I'm going to go talk to this man of your aunt's that you didn't tell me about. Watch the fire."

I nodded and sat on the stool near the stove. I placed one elbow on my knee and my chin on my palm, thinking about the mystery of love. Jian's hair did indeed curl at the ends, and he seemed smart. I was not used to new people, though, and found his politeness strange. My grandmother disliked that Jian had showed up with a gift of chocolate.

I heard her tell my mother that a man shouldn't have to bring bribes to gain affection.

Jian's voice carried from the living room to my perch in the kitchen. "My family is nomadic, so when I want to go home for a visit, I write a letter two and a half months ahead of time. The post office dispatches a man who knows the last place my family camped at and he rides in that direction. If he passes other nomadic families, he might give the letter to one of them. Eventually, the letter finds my family, and my father comes to the train station on the day of my return with fresh horses. Then we ride a few days to where they are. The area around the train station is turning into a city, whose outskirts sprawl into places we used to herd horses and sheep. Every time I return home, the ride is longer and longer. If I don't have enough days of holiday in a row, I can't visit."

"Oh, what a terrible way to live," my mother said.

My father and uncles laughed.

"It's what they are used to," Jian said. "My family could never live here. It's too cold. They would freeze half the year."

I shivered and moved closer to the fire. The metal grill acted as a radiator, so that I felt the heat in mellow waves. I drifted. My elbow slid off my knee a few times. *Sleepy. Must keep the fire alive.*

It's not going to die. If it does, I'll know because it will get cold. I fell asleep into a world of deserts and horses, filled with sunlight and air that shimmered heat.

"Wake up! Wake up!" Ainara yelled, jumping up and down, the fine earth on the floor billowing around her feet.

I opened one eye a crack and screamed. A spark had escaped the grate and ignited the new shirt my mother had sewn for me. The fire ate a tiny hole that grew as I flailed and hit myself in the chest, until I finally smothered it.

My mother rushed in. "*Aiyah*, Aimee! How could you be so careless, child?"

"It was so cold and I tried to get closer to the grate, then I fell asleep. But only for a second"—I pointed at my chest—"and now I'm naked!"

My mother patted my head. "I'll patch it."

"Maybe it could be a new style," said Jian from the doorway.

I frowned. I didn't want to be the only child in school whose new shirt was already patched.

My mother said, "The good news is the fire didn't go out, so our fish stew is done and we can eat. You did a good job, Aimee."

I couldn't help but smile.

We soon crowded around the dining table, some sitting staggered in a second row, others on the *kang* bed so that we all fit.

In addition to the fish stew, there were dumplings, stir-fried beef with preserved vegetables, Chinese cabbage with wood ear mushrooms, whole chicken in ginseng broth, blackened pork hocks in soy sauce, peanuts fried in sugared oil, snow fungus soup and white rice.

My uncles toasted my grandmother. Jian raised a glass and thanked my family. And so it went, warm wishes and toasts throughout the night. I concentrated on eating the best morsels and hardly said a word.

After dinner, the adults told stories. My mother's specialty was Manchu folktales. Everyone knew them, but because she told them with such passion and changed them each time—with fresh characters, new beginnings, different endings—we were always happy to listen.

Ainara tossed a frozen persimmon at me, but I missed catching it and it hit me in the ribs. In winter all the fruit was frozen, whether we wanted it that way or not.

My mother had been watching. "Come on, you two." She led us to the kitchen, where she filled an enamel bowl with water. She floated the frozen persimmon in the bowl, along with some others.

I stuck my hand in the water and immediately pulled it back. "It's cold!"

My mother poked a persimmon and sent it sailing across the bowl. "Of course it is. Hot water would cook the outside before the fruit thawed. The cold water draws the ice out so it can be eaten faster."

"How fast?" I asked.

"About half an hour."

"Half an hour? I want one now." I pushed a persimmon against the bowl with a finger, and it clinked against the side. "We'll keep watch. You go chat with the other adults."

Ainara tugged on my arm. "But I want to listen to Mother's stories."

"Stay here with me."

As soon as our mother disappeared into the living room, I grabbed a persimmon and laid it on the counter. I picked up the cleaver and brought it down hard. Thin petals of ice shattered off the exterior, but the cleaver didn't penetrate.

I placed the persimmon back in the bowl and tried another. After three persimmons, the tips of my fingers froze and we were no closer to a treat.

I shrugged. "I guess we wait."

Twenty minutes later, I succeeded in chopping a persimmon into quarters. The thin orange skin tore easily under the blade, but the flesh took effort to separate.

Ainara poked the flesh. "It has pieces inside like an orange."

"Those are the persimmon's tongues. It's a noisy fruit."

"It has so many. Animals only have one tongue." She stuck her tongue out. "See?"

"But it's not an animal, it's a persimmon. They have many tongues and that's the fun." Ainara was a year younger than me, and I so enjoyed being knowledgeable in front of her that I made up facts. "If you eat many persimmons, you will speak many languages."

"Really?" Ainara stuck a piece into her mouth and spoke around it. "Why would I want to speak many languages?"

I chewed a piece of the fruit. The tongues were still frozen, their half-moon shape not discernible until the heat of our mouths melted the ice. "Because when we leave home, we'll have to speak many languages to the people we meet."

Ainara grimaced. "I think I'll just stay here."

"Ow." I drew air through my teeth to quell the icy pain from the half-frozen fruit. "Many things are painful at first, but later you may see that you grew because of the pain."

FOUR

I got emergency visas and tickets for a flight that left early the next morning.

After I got home, I dialed my sister's number again. The phone rang once, twice, before a little girl answered. "Hello?" It must be Lien, my sister's daughter. She was born after I'd left for America, so I'd never met her.

"Hello," I said. My voice splintered and popped as it traveled over the line. "Can you hear me?"

"Hello, hello, hello," she sang.

Words failed me, sound failed me, technology failed me. I wanted to say, "Is your mother home?" or "Is your dad there?" or "It's your aunt Aimee!"

The line died.

If I couldn't even find words to talk to a little girl on the phone, facing my entire family in person would be a disaster.

I breathed deep and dialed again.

The phone rang and rang, but no one picked up.

I mouthed the words silently, first in English, then in Chinese: *I'm coming home. Wait for me, Mother, wait for me.*

I slipped into bed, careful not to wake David, who had fallen asleep. I lay flat on my back, arms at my sides and palms up, hoping that sleep would embrace my ready form. The neighborhood sounds of engines and sirens ebbed like the end of a waltz. My eyes closed and my breathing slowed. Memories played out before me, scenes from a thousand movies melded together. And played. And played.

Still awake, I turned and stared at the red glow of the alarm clock that read 1:34:08. I watched the seconds, counting away. A minute is a long time if you watch each second.

Days are long. Life is short. The time since I'd left Eternal Spring, a lifetime.

I turned to face David and laid a hand on his shoulder. I wanted to talk to him, to fill the silence and quell the fears. We'd met freshman year and argued over Prometheus in the one literature class he took as an elective. He said that talking to me helped him see the world more clearly. His eyes scanned rapidly beneath his eyelids, lost in REM.

Finally, I got up and dressed in some clothes from a pile on the floor. Whenever I took off a piece of clothing, I was disciplined enough to throw it into a pile of similar colors, then kick-roll the bundle to maintain its shape. But I usually didn't touch it again until my waves of discarded clothing evolved into tsunamis.

So, the night before my fourteen-hour flight into my past, I did laundry. I didn't want to wake David with the noise of our washer-dryer, so I wrapped bundles in sheets and hauled them hobo-style two blocks to the twenty-four-hour laundromat. The night air was growing teeth, and the bakers out on their smoking breaks catcalled my insanity.

It didn't take long enough to wash, dry and fold everything into color-coded stacks, then haul it home.

With the laundry gone, the walking spaces of our apartment had grown. Patches of hardwood floor appeared, the finish unmarred by human feet, but the rest of the place was still stuffed full. Shelves stacked vertically then horizontally with books, piles of research papers and magazines on the coffee table, parts for solar panels next to the couch. My collection of purses and shoes topped the bookshelves. Teapots shaped like peacocks and elephants and ladybugs fought for space on all the horizontal surfaces with pillar candles, scented candles in jars with metal lids, and candle sculptures of the Greek gods. Videocassettes, laser discs and CDs. Folios of photographs, boxes of broken camera bits, picture frames I'd never filled.

My eyes landed on a purple leather purse I'd bought three years ago because I loved the color. I'd never used it. A yellow Post-it on the handle read "Donate?" It was my handwriting, but I'd forgotten writing it. Next to the purse stood a candle I'd never lit. In my childhood, we used to study by candlelight. Now they were an aspiration of tranquility never realized—the apartment a fire hazard.

I never used the teapots for making tea. I drank coffee.

Usually, my things made me feel cozy. Rich. My childhood years of material deprivation were behind me and I had moved forward, into a new and better place. Tonight, I felt suffocated.

There was so much of it that we didn't invite anyone over except our closest friends.

Stuff occupies the same space as people.

I fetched some garbage bags from under the kitchen sink and filled them: candles, vases, piggy banks, purses, movies we'd watched but hadn't enjoyed, CDs I'd bought then regretted, yoga mats in different colors. I searched the junk drawer for a Sharpie and wrote "Donate" on the bags, then tied each one off with an exhale.

I loaded the recycling bins with sales flyers, magazines, restaurant receipts, soda bottles and cans, shopping bags and shoe boxes.

I took another garbage bag around the apartment and filled it with broken camera parts, teacups with cracked handles, and everything else I shouldn't have owned, let alone kept.

I only bagged things that belonged to me, and in doing so I realized how little of our stuff had been accumulated by David. He had grown up with money and never seemed to need anything. Or perhaps knowing that he could buy things when needed lent him a certain freedom.

When I finished I still felt heavy, but no longer as if I might sink through the crust of the earth.

"DAVID," I SAID, coming into the room and sitting on the bed next to him. "Rise and shine."

"What?" His lashes parted.

"We have to catch a plane." I gripped the bottom edge of the comforter and pulled.

He curled his fingers into the top border to halt its progress. "But planes fly so fast."

"Yes, that's why we have to hurry."

David sat up, rubbed his eyes and was immediately awake. He was dressed and ready to go fifteen minutes later. His morning magic never ceased to amaze—and slightly annoy—me.

I triple-checked again that we had our passports and plane tickets.

He nodded at the color-coded clothes in our closet. "Seems the laundry fairy was here last night." But when he entered the living room, his smile disappeared. "What happened?"

I shrugged. "I couldn't sleep. You're always saying we have too much stuff." I followed him across the empty floor, pulling my suitcase.

He turned to face me at the door. "Yes, but this borders on—"

"I didn't throw out your stuff or anything that you gave me." I nodded at a bookshelf from which I had excavated the paperbacks. I'd filled it instead with his football memorabilia. An autographed photo of Walter Payton and other Chicago Bears smiled at David's vinyl album of "The Super Bowl Shuffle." His father was a sports nut, and David had grown up playing football, baseball and basketball.

He smiled then and kissed me on the forehead. "How do you know I didn't love the rhinoceros teapot?"

"We never had a rhino teapot. We had an elephant and a hippo."

"Right." He was looking at me with more than his usual warm concern.

I took a deep breath. "I realized I hadn't thrown anything out the entire time I've been in America. Why was I holding on to it all?"

"You must have had your reasons."

I'd been thinking about my mother so much, her habit of telling a story instead of giving a straight answer had invaded me. I mimed the movements as I spoke. "My grandmother once had a green coat, made of wool. When the edges of the sleeves became threadbare, she added new cuffs and cut it down into a jacket for my mother. When the elbows grew thin, my mother patched them, then tucked in the hem and shortened the sleeves for me to wear. Eventually, my mother cut along the seams and used the fabric of the front and back to make a pair of pants for my sister. We didn't have much, so we never threw anything away."

I pulled on a new jacket I'd bought a year ago but never worn.

David frowned. "You go from never throwing anything away to throwing away half your things. Won't you miss some of it?" He lifted the ladybug teapot from a bag marked for donation and set it on the entryway table.

I hoisted my purse over one shoulder and my camera over the other. "Maybe it's time for me to change."

"Wait, you've still got—" He grabbed my arm and ripped the price tag from the sleeve of my jacket. He smiled, and a lock of hair fell over his forehead. When I brushed it back, I noticed a white hair mixed in with the blond. "Hey, you have a white hair."

He smiled. "It's the next step. There are no blond mad scientists. I need white hair that stands on end, like Newton, Einstein, Doc Brown."

I smiled, then felt guilty for the way that even in the depths of misery, small joys intrude on the heart.

Heart, *xin*.

Xiao xin—small heart—means to be careful. *Cao xin* means to worry. My mother used to say, "Worrying is wishing for something you don't want, so why worry?"

WE ARRIVED AT the gate for our flight unusually early.

My legs felt wooden and I leaned against David. He kissed the top of my head. "You can sleep on the flight. I know this isn't the best way for me to take my first trip to China, but I want to see this village you're from, where the sunlight is always pink."

"Rose."

"Even better."

"It's from dust storms."

"You don't need to dispel the illusion. Hey, isn't that one of yours?" David pointed at a poster advertising a bank in which a man and a woman pushed a boy on a swing in Central Park.

"Yes. It is from two years ago, in January. I remember there was a snowstorm that day."

David was still staring at the photo. He had brought up the subject of children when we married, but I'd told him I wanted to wait. I'd never specified what I was waiting for.

"A perfect family," he said at last.

I nodded. But they weren't a family. They were models from different agencies. Each arrived separately in the studio with snow in their hair. They introduced themselves to one another, then turned to the camera as a unit. Joe had set up gold reflectors to bounce warm light onto their faces to replicate sunshine. A week later, a digital artist added Central Park as the background.

They were strangers thrust together for a moment, but they were the image of a happy family.

FIVE

I kept my dream of leaving Eternal Spring a secret for seven years, from my eighth birthday, when I'd fallen into the photograph, to the day when I was fifteen and received a letter that would change my life.

When my mother had picked up my portrait, she'd bought me a print of the photo of New York as well. I was so happy that I ignored the image of myself riding a bicycle in a lake and fell into the one of New York again and again. Once, I stayed too long because I was so entranced I didn't want to return home.

I fell into a photo of Yen's family at Chinese New Year too. Basically, any photo and every photo I saw. But they were all of people and places I knew intimately. The photo of New York City was special.

I imagined it as a place only the intrepid, the few, the special could reach. You had to recognize that you belonged there before you ever set foot on its pavement. You had to deserve to be there, and it in turn would deserve you.

Eternal Spring was too small to contain me.

Aunt Eyun told me about a boarding high school in Harbin that accepted students based on merit. They didn't care about the applicant's residency paper—the single sheet assigned at birth that tied each Chinese person to a particular village or town or city.

I studied hard and got good grades. In my final year of middle school, when I had to take exams for high school, Aunt Eyun mailed me an application.

The day my acceptance letter arrived, I waited until everyone was finished eating dinner.

"I have an announcement," I said in my perkiest tone, hoping my view of this development would carry the day.

My grandmother chuckled. "Another perfect test score?"

My father smiled. "Where are the bonus points?"

"And the points for form and neat handwriting?" Ainara asked.

My mother and sister laughed, dancing candlelight reflected in their eyes.

"No, it's not a perfect test score. I received an acceptance letter today from a high school in Harbin. It's wonderful news!"

"Congratulations!" Ainara said, rolling her chopsticks back and forth on the table.

My mother asked, "What do you mean you've been accepted to a high school in Harbin?"

"I applied a few months ago. I have a full scholarship, and it's a boarding school. I don't even have to pay for food."

"That's good, considering you're always hungry," my sister said. She opened her mouth to say more, but then looked at my mother and closed it.

"How much time?" my mother asked.

How much time since I'd applied, how much time since I'd received the acceptance letter, how much time until I went away, or how much time until I returned? What did she mean? "I got the letter today."

My mother crossed her arms as if to hug herself. "How much time since you came up with the idea of going to school in Harbin?"

"A few years."

"Years! Years I've spent thinking I was a good mother." It was strange that she thought it was about her being good or bad, and not about me and my ambitions.

"You *are* a good mother," Ainara insisted.

"Then how did I not know my eldest daughter has been planning to leave me?"

I winced. *I'm not leaving just you, I'm leaving everyone. Everything.* "I didn't say anything because what would be the point if I failed?"

My mother nodded. "Of course, it's a great accomplishment, and I'm proud of you. But you can't go."

"Why not? I thought all Chinese parents want the best for their children."

"I want that for you too. I just want the best for you here."

"Eternal Spring is too small. There's nothing here."

My mother shook her head. "*We're* here. You're safe here."

"There's no university here. No museums or art galleries. The high school in Harbin has labs, teachers, a library full of thousands of books."

My mother would not meet my eyes. "We also have teachers and thousands of stories. Ours are just not published." She was right—she had told me countless stories. But I was more interested in permanence, in words that could be written and photos that could be printed. I was interested in the immortality of art.

At last, my father said, "Good for you. One of my children gets to leave."

My grandmother closed her eyes. When she opened them again, stress wrinkles pulled at her temples.

My father scanned the scarred tabletop, as if searching for a particular line. "When you go to the city, you'll get a temporary Harbin residency permit. If you do well, they may give you a permanent one."

"I've always had an Eternal Spring residency permit," my mother said. "I've never wanted to live anywhere else."

He ignored her and continued. "If you test well in Harbin, maybe you'll get into a university in Beijing. Then you can try to get a Beijing residency permit. You won't have to come back."

I shook my head, making believe I would be back after high school. My heart knew I was lying.

My mother gripped the table. "You can't go to Harbin."

Anger and desperation and futility flared inside me.

My mother's hands formed fists. "Eyun's too busy to take care of you. You won't know anybody. There will be no family or neighbors or friends to protect you. It's too dangerous for a young girl."

My father cupped one of her fists, leaning toward her. "You've never lived anywhere else. How would you know?"

My mother pulled away. "I don't want to hear you refry that all over again."

I frowned at my parents and grandmother, but no one explained. My mother told many stories, but they were stories about other people, not herself.

Her voice was a plea. "You're my eldest daughter."

"Ainara will be here for you."

Ainara nodded. "I'm not going anywhere."

My mother smiled at her, then turned to face me. "I want you both to be here."

I quoted the story of the Nishan shaman, aware I was using my mother's own words against her. "Sergudai was fifteen when he made up his mind to go hunting on Ice Dragon Mountain. I'm fifteen—"

"He fell ill with fever and died. Also, Sergudai was a son. Daughters are different. Far worse things can happen to a daughter than to a son."

"It's a boarding school. The school will take care of me and be my parent. You always say China is like a parent—"

"Don't you like it here with us?" My mother raised her hands as if to hold me, then let them drop into her lap.

I reached for her but she leaned back, a gesture that hurt me as much as a slap across the face. "Of course, I do. It's home. But I may like it better somewhere else. I won't know until I've tried."

My mother sighed and took Ainara's hand. "I won't allow you to go, Aimee. I'm sorry. You need parental permission."

I had never imagined a single moment could separate us. "Father will sign."

She looked to him for support.

He nodded, eyes on the tabletop once more. "I will sign."

My mother threw up her hands with a shout and left the house. Ainara hurried after her. My father patted my shoulder, then he too went after my mother.

SIX

After fourteen hours on the plane—twenty-six hours if you counted the time difference—we landed in China.

The new Beijing airport resembled a cathedral, the ceiling rising to meet in an apex of steel-vaulted ribs. Walking away from the gate was like striding under the wings of an angel.

The air snapped with a sense of possibility, from the polished marble walls to the welcoming mural at the end of the escalator. The citizens in the mural all faced the sunrise, their hopeful, ruddy cheeks offset by bleached-tooth smiles. Instead of Chairman Mao's Little Red Book, they held briefcases, paintbrushes, hammers, CPUs.

Posters lined the corridors advertising the coming Moon Festival. "It's my mother's favorite festival," I told David as we made our way to customs and immigration. "Every year there was a light competition in our village. My father always gathered whatever materials he could and built a lantern."

David studied a photo of an octagonal lantern as we walked past. "I bet I'd be good at that." He pointed to a poster on the opposite wall and chuckled. "Does that actually say 'Embrace Profit'?"

A man held a bank ledger in one hand and a basket of fish in the other. Red words flew in the sky above his head, in both Chinese and English. "It actually does."

"How are you holding up?"

"I'm standing. That's something, right?"

"And walking too, so that's good."

I nodded.

We cleared customs and immigration with few words and no incidents. The officer's alert eyes compared us to our photos and stamped the passports with resounding thumps.

The baggage carousel's metallic waves folded, crashing forward but never reaching shore, piled with suitcases and duffel bags, cardboard boxes wrapped in cellophane, wooden crates strapped with yellow rope. Everyone had brought gifts for family and friends. I felt guilty, waiting for my one suitcase stuffed with nothing but my own clothes and toiletries.

We were the last two people standing at the carousel when it stopped turning.

I half sighed, half groaned. We followed signs to the lost luggage counter. A woman in a navy uniform and pillbox hat looked us up and down, then said hello in English, enunciating each syllable.

I blinked and said, "*Ni hao*," hello in Chinese. My pronunciation sounded hard-edged even to my ears. Mandarin Chinese tasted strange in my mouth. In my brain.

I had learned English so well it had become the language of my thoughts. I had to first think in English, then translate into Chinese.

She smiled and responded in Chinese. "How may I help you?"

I placed my purse and camera on the counter. People to our left and right jostled for space to fill out paperwork. "I lost something." I mimed a rectangle, not able to remember the word for luggage. "This big, black. From New York, flight 561."

She handed me a triplicate carbon form and said in English, "Fill out."

I filled it out. The woman read my answers, made a few notations, then handed me the faintest of the copies. "A-OK, we will find what you are missing."

She handed me a manila envelope. I peeked inside: a toothbrush, toothpaste, a comb and a cotton handkerchief.

When I thanked her, she said, "No need for thanks."

David whispered, "You did want to have less stuff."

I glared at him, and he laughed.

Outside the frosted sliding doors was the China I remembered, an ocean of people with black hair and brown eyes, who blurred together into an unnerving wall.

I squinted at them, but they became no clearer.

A camera iris focuses by narrowing the lens to make objects sharp. I held up my left thumb and forefinger, then touched them to the top of my right forefinger, forming a tiny triangle, a pinhole camera. I held it up to my left eye and closed the right one. People snapped into focus.

They looked expectant, searched for a friend or a relative or something less tangible. Their eyes touched us and shot away again. We were not what any of them were waiting for.

"Are you all right?" David asked.

I managed a smile. "I must be tired from all the cleaning and laundry, and you know, not sleeping."

I wanted to take a photo of the crowd to study the people it contained more closely, but when I felt for the comfort of my camera on my hip, it was gone.

"Where's my camera?" I had my purse, which meant I still had my identification. But without my camera I didn't have my identity.

"Come on," David said. "Let's retrace our steps."

A different woman in navy uniform and pillbox hat was at the counter.

I spoke in English, reverting to the language of my thoughts in my distress. "I lost my camera on the counter just now. I put it down to fill out paperwork. Then, when I left, I must've not have picked it up again."

She pursed her lips. "You abandoned it."

It felt like an accusation. How could I abandon a part of myself? "We just got off a long flight. I haven't slept—"

"It was costly, the camera?"

I nodded. "I'd be happy to offer a reward. It's worth more than money."

She frowned, as if I had argued light was darkness and darkness, light. "You do not understand. No one ever finds anything costly."

I sighed and left my contact info, in case someone did find my camera and chose to return it. The woman's lips twitched, but the smile did not reach her eyes.

I thanked her, and she said, "No need to thank."

David held my hand as we walked again through the wall of strangers into the arrivals area. I glanced at our reflection in a curving mirrored wall and was consumed by the need to photograph the couple with unruly hair and sunken eyes who stared back at me.

While I checked on our connecting flight to Harbin, David bought me a disposable camera from an airport store. I clutched its cardboard and plastic body the way a lost child hugs a doll.

SEVEN

There would be no flight to Harbin. The airline had canceled it and was rebooking the passengers. Because of the lost luggage and then the lost camera, we were the last ones to be assigned tickets. Our flight would be three days later.

I glared at the ticket agent. "We have to get to Harbin to—"

She cut me off in a monotone. "Because of the high volume of travelers during the holiday, availability of seats is very tight."

"Of course. The Moon Festival." All of the posters in the airport. My mother's favorite. "Are there seats on another airline?"

She sniffed. "No, not in my system. You might try the train."

Exhausted, I found a travel agency inside the airport. All of the seats on the express train had sold out. The local would stop at many towns whose names sounded familiar, lyrics from a mostly forgotten song. It would take eleven hours to deliver us to Harbin. All of the plush first-class seats were sold out, and only the second class "medium-hard" seating remained. I bought two.

When I told David, he said "Fantastic," in a tone that indicated it was anything but.

❦

ON THE TRAIN, the three people whose row faced ours were a man, a woman and a boy. The boy greeted us by hiding in his mother's skirt. The man nodded at David, then at me, and buried his face in a newspaper.

David bounced on the seat. "This isn't bad. Medium-hard seating in China beats the hell out of Amtrak."

"What did the foreigner say?" the woman asked me.

"He said these seats are more comfortable than on the trains in America."

"What did she say?" David asked.

"She asked me what you said, and I told her."

"What did he say?" the woman asked.

I sighed.

David's Chinese vocabulary included the names of his favorite foods, *ni hao* for hello, *wo ai ni* for I love you, and *zhong guo* for China. The only full sentence he could speak was, "Hello, I love you, China."

"*Ni hao.*" He waved to the woman and the boy. His *ni* was too deep and his *hao* too long, but they understood and seemed delighted at his effort.

"Say hello to the nice man and his translator," the woman said to her son.

"Hello, Auntie." The boy called me Auntie in the way Chinese children call all women Big Sister or Auntie.

"Hello, it's nice to meet you. But I'm not his translator. I'm his wife."

"*Aiyah*, my mistake." She pointed at him. "That's even better—such a handsome husband."

I translated for David. He smiled at her and patted himself on the chest.

The boy whispered to his mother, and she said, "Your accent is northeastern, but you sound harsh, like you haven't spoken in a long time."

I nodded. I was beginning to think in both Chinese and English, like listening to two radio stations at once. After a pause to sort myself out, I said, "I've been overseas for a long time. In the United States."

"New York, New York!" the boy sang in English, his shyness evaporating.

David gave him a thumbs-up, and the boy blushed.

"So you're home visiting." She directed her gaze at David. "Your parents must be so proud."

"Yes, I'm home for a visit."

We were cast into darkness as the train traveled through a tunnel out of the city and into the countryside. In the blackness, I could see things more clearly. I thought about the lies we tell strangers and the lies we tell ourselves.

Out the other end of the tunnel, David searched through his backpack and found a stress ball. It was an earth printed with the continents and the logo of his company, Prometheus Solar. It fit perfectly in the boy's hand. The boy's face lit up as he threw the ball hard against the floor. It bounced not at all.

David gestured for the ball, then demonstrated it was for squeezing not bouncing. The boy laughed and happily deformed the continents.

"Are you from Harbin?" the woman asked.

"Near Harbin. A village called Eternal Spring."

"Oh, Eternal Spring! Of course. When you said village, I thought maybe one of those tiny places where there was no electricity until the 1980s. Eternal Spring's not a village. My cousin moved there to work in the oil fields."

I translated for David as she spoke but felt the need to correct her. "There was no electricity in Eternal Spring when I was a child. The public buildings got it in 1986, and then it took another year to get it into the houses."

The woman seemed glad for the chance to impress us with her knowledge. "Shows how fast China's developing, doesn't it? Imagine! Thirteen years ago there were no electricity lines, and now people have solar panels on their roofs."

I translated for David and he asked whether they were using glass-backed or polymer-based solar panels, and the efficiency percentages.

The woman laughed. "I just know my cousin says electricity used to come from coal, then from oil, and now it comes from the sun. It's amazing how fast things change."

I translated again for David. He scribbled something on a Post-it Note and stuck it back inside his backpack.

"It's interesting that they're drilling for oil but using solar for power."

I shrugged. "Planning for the future, I guess."

The woman peeled an orange and offered us sections. "How long since you were last home?"

I shook my head. "Too long."

"It always feels that way, whether it's a month or a year. It's been six months since we've been back. Time goes so fast, especially when you have a child to care for." She hugged the boy to her side. He poked at the North Pole, giggling as it sank into the oceans.

"And a husband."

"No husband. Just us."

Startled, I looked at the man next to her, who was now sleeping, his head propped against the headrest. She waved her hand without looking. "He's not with us."

"I'm sorry. Did your husband die?"

She laughed so hard tears formed at the corners of her eyes, leaning to swat at my arm in mirth. "No, though some days I wish he would! We're divorced." She said it as casually as she'd said Eternal Spring was not a village.

When I left China, ten years ago, I took a mental snapshot of the country, of the way it looked, the way it felt, the way people behaved. In the time I was gone, China had evolved, and so had her people. A face seen every day remains the same, but a face seen rarely ages dramatically. A photo of China now would show me something entirely different.

The train jolted and picked up speed. I leaned over David in the window seat. When I raised the camera to my eye, the shot would have been of a field. By the time I clicked the shutter, the photo was of a high-rise building.

ELEVEN HOURS LATER, as the sky turned to dusk, the overhead speakers announced our impending arrival in Harbin. Passengers grasped their bags and crowded the center aisle, the heat of strange bodies pressing in from every side. David braced his elbows on the chair backs on either side of the aisle and caged me in, as if he were afraid I'd be crushed. The train rocked harder from side to side as we neared the station, wheels screaming.

"Harbin," he whispered, like it was the first half of the word *harbinger*.

"It's actually three words," I said. "Pronounced Ha-R-Bin. It's known as the 'city of ice,' but my mother told me Harbin is Manchu for a place to dry fishing nets."

David lifted a brow. "Frozen fishing nets?"

"It isn't a city of ice all year round. Just most of the year."

"But your village is called Eternal Spring."

"It is."

"So how can it be near the city of ice?"

I shrugged. "The founders had a sense of humor. Eternal Spring is farther northeast, and even colder. I could practically see Siberia and North Korea from the roof of our school."

With a final screech, the train stopped.

David and I were carried forward on the tide of bodies. Once we hit the platform, I walked faster and faster trying to uncramp my legs from their hours of stagnation. David, with his longer legs, had no trouble keeping up.

A man sat hunched at the bus transportation desk, counting ticket stubs. His forefingers wore stains of black ink.

"Thirty-six, thirty-eight, forty, forty-two. Good, good." He secured the stubs with an elastic band, then looked up. "How can I help?"

"Two tickets to Eternal Spring, please."

The man's gray chin beard quivered as he spoke. "Eternal Spring? Ah, Miss. It just left." He gestured to the street outside.

"How long ago?"

He checked a schedule on his desk, then peered at his watch. "Twenty-one minutes ago. The next one will be in ten hours and thirty-nine minutes."

I blinked. I thought I heard a cricket chirp in laughter. "You mean, tomorrow?"

"Yes, tomorrow."

"There's nothing sooner?"

He clucked and spoke in a drumbeat baritone. "There is. It left twenty-two minutes ago."

More cricket chirping. "Is there any other way of getting to Eternal Spring right now?"

"Not unless you can fly."

I cheered up, hope lifting me from my aching body. "There are flights from here?"

He chuckled. "I meant, unless you could flap your arms very fast, like wings." He raised his eyebrows and whispered, "You can't, can you?"

My shoulders slumped and the cricket laughed again.

I was going mad.

David leaned into my ear. "Do you hear a cricket?"

I nodded. We were both going mad.

The ticket seller whispered, "What did the foreigner say?"

"He asked if I heard a cricket."

The ticket seller smiled and, with a deft turn of his wrist, drew from his sleeve an intricately carved rosewood box pierced with air holes. As David and I moved closer, he slid the top open to reveal a lime-green cricket.

The cricket's antenna twitched as it turned in the box, tasting new air. The ticket seller drew a chopstick from his other sleeve. A wooden carving of a cricket was impaled on one end.

He coaxed the cricket out of its box onto the desk and shimmied the carved cricket in front of it. "When you fight a real cricket with a fake cricket and the real one always wins, then he becomes used to winning and will be more confident and braver when he fights other real crickets."

He paused to stare first at me, then at David.

I translated as the crickets battled.

"If the real cricket always loses to the fake cricket, when he goes into a real match, he will be less confident and more likely to lose."

I translated again.

"But he cannot win every match. It is impossible." The fight finished in what I understood to be a draw. The ticket seller lifted the lime-green cricket on his finger and placed it back in its box. "The next bus to Eternal Spring leaves in ten hours and thirty-six minutes."

I copied his staccato rhythm for David as I bought the tickets. "The bus to Eternal Spring will leave in ten hours and now thirty-five minutes."

The ticket seller waved us on.

As we walked away to the sound of cricket echoes, David hugged me to his side. "Let's get a room and find some food." He touched the shadows under my eyes. "You need some sleep."

HARBIN WAS A city that lived in the east but looked like the west. When I first came here for high school, I was surprised by the Russian cathedrals and Georgian houses. Now I was struck by the Chinese temples and pagodas—at once familiar yet strange.

"Has it changed much?" David asked as we walked down the cobblestone street.

"Nighttime used to be dark here: you could see stars. But now there are so many bright storefronts." I could read the names of shops from across the street, but the smaller signs and advertising blurred until they could have been written in English, Chinese or Manchu.

"I'm sorry," I said. "I wish you could see it as if on holiday. But I'm so out of it I—"

"Amy? Shut up."

"What?"

He tapped his ear. "Shut up and listen."

Sound poured from every open doorway, Beijing opera and English pop songs clashing for attention. A Viennese waltz danced out of a park nearby and David pulled me toward it.

Red lanterns limned in gold hung from every lamppost. The park teemed with people in clothing of all different designs. After decades of color and pattern existing only for the benefit of children, adults had embraced fashion to the extreme.

A woman in a fuchsia *qipao* slit up to the thigh ran past, holding hands with her twin sister, dressed in a black lace gown whose hem floated above the ground. I tugged on David's hand, and we followed them.

Women in silk-embroidered vests strolled the walkways as clusters of men wearing neon and pastel shirts played chess. Vendors with food carts sold steamed dumplings, barbecued lamb on skewers, and dragon's beard cotton candy; steam, smoke and powder climbed the air, entwined together.

A symphony orchestra nested in the trees. The horns and percussion rode broad limbs, while the first violin stood jauntily astride two branches. The legs of the piano stretched toward the earth, while the branches of the oak tree reached up—lovers holding hands. Tendrils of nearby weeping willows rippled to the music.

Beyond the orchestra was a square, and in the square were hundreds of people.

Dancing.

They moved as if with one breath, men and women, elderly and toddlers, teenagers, mothers holding babies.

The edge of the dancing mass shimmered, then absorbed the women we followed. A heart beating, a wave swelling, they danced on.

David held up my hand, asking my permission to join in.

I saw a woman in profile for a split second before she disappeared into the dancing heart of the crowd. She looked familiar. I dropped David's hand and chased after her. I caught glares and elbows as I pursued. Soon I stopped fighting, swaying to the music, and that's when I caught up with her.

I tapped her on the shoulder.

She turned and smiled at me, a young woman who may have resembled my mother as she had been years before I was born. She took my hand, and we waltzed to a song without words. I had so much I wanted to say to her, my mother. Words coalesced and dissolved in my mind, but none made it past my lips.

Someone tapped me on the shoulder from behind, and I looked around. David had found me. When I turned back, the woman was gone.

"Why did you run off?" He sounded upset—a rare state for David.

I shook my head. "I don't know. Everything's surreal."

"Let's get some food," he said, and I followed him out of the dancing throng.

We walked along a street hung with lanterns for the Moon Festival, their oval red bodies and gold tassels waving in the breeze. The closest restaurant featured murals of the Venice canals. Steam sashayed from the open door of the kitchen, scenting the air with garlic and butter.

At the next table, a woman complained, "But I wanted real foreign food. Italian pasta is just Chinese noodles. We exported it years ago, and they sent it back to us with a different name."

Our bowls of noodles arrived.

Something Manchu, something Chinese, exported many years ago as Aimee, was now back as Amy.

EIGHT

When I was a child, my favorite holiday changed with the seasons—in the winter it was Chinese New Year, in the summer the Dragon Boat Festival. My mother's favorite was eternal: the Moon Festival.

The week before the festival, the bakery made mooncakes, round pastries with sweet fillings of red beans or lotus seeds. Fancy mooncakes contained an egg yolk inside; even fancier ones, the yolk of an egg that was not quite a baby chick. Those were crunchy, and Grandfather Feng loved them. Sometimes, after he finished eating one, he'd smile with tiny feathers caught in his front teeth, the cat that ate the bird in the cage, gleeful and victorious.

My mother told me a story about the Moon Festival. "There was a Manchu girl whose greatest love was for a celestial being who lived on the moon. Every year during the Moon Festival, a magical bridge forms between the moon and the earth and they can be together for just one day."

I thought it was romantic.

While my mother loved the stories, my father loved the lights strung along our street and through the trees, the lights that shone from paper lanterns and the candles floating down the River of Stories to guide the spirits of the dead. Every year, my father helped hang the village lights.

He spent his spare time depicting the world around him. He owned a bound sketchbook, half-full of detailed drawings of never-realized buildings and portraits of people in the village, the rest blank.

On the last day of every month, he would sit with me and Ainara and slice out three pages with a razor. Blank paper was a luxury, so on these pages we never created anything less than a masterpiece. My father's ruler and homemade T-square helped us draw perfect angles in pencil.

We would count on the fingers of each hand the days of the week and their corresponding numbers, ensuring that August always ended on a thirty-first and February did not, then draw a grid, pausing to write Monday, Tuesday and so on across the top. Ainara drew trees and flowers and pagodas with colored pencils. I drew the sun and the moon and my father's high-rise buildings.

After two or three hours of toil, we would each have an illustrated calendar of the coming month, on which we marked the activities we would do together on which days: calligraphy on Mondays, painting on Tuesdays, martial arts on Wednesdays, singing and harmonica playing on alternating Thursdays, philosophy on Fridays, poetry on Saturdays, sculpture on Sundays.

This was of course in addition to six days a week of school and homework, then helping around the house all day Sunday. We would pin our calendars on the wall and stand back in admiration.

One evening, my father found me as I was playing with Yen in the yard. Yen's parents had bought him a metal toy helicopter with rotating blades. He flew it only once before we opened it with a screwdriver to learn how it worked, but after we closed the body back up, I still held one screw in my palm.

"This year, I'm going to make the best lantern anyone in this village has ever seen," my father said.

I thought he was a great artist and was always eager to help him. "Can I help? I will help you win!"

Yen stuck his hand up as if in class. "Me too! I want to help you make the best lantern."

"Of course, you can both help." My father laughed, but he was not altogether merry. "I can't do it without help, and I doubt anyone else will volunteer."

"We'll show them all," I said.

"Yes, we will."

"So, what are we going to make?" Yen asked.

"It's a secret. You both have to promise not to tell anyone." My father looked right then left in the fading light, leaned in close, and whispered.

I laughed in delight. "Oh, that's a great idea. That will win for sure!"

"Of course it will, because we'll make it together."

My father confiscated a corner of the food storage shed. It would have been full of Chinese cabbage and potatoes in winter, but in summer, we ate fresh vegetables, so there was space for him to work. He acted the part of mad scientist for the month it took us to assemble his design, opening the door a crack to let me and Yen enter with supplies, glaring suspiciously to ensure we hadn't been observed or followed.

❦

WHEN MY AUNT Eyun came home for that Moon Festival, Jian did not come with her.

She dropped her bag on the *kang* bed.

"Aunt Eyun, Father and Yen and I have made an entry for the lantern competition. It's a secret, so I can't tell you what it is, but it's great."

"Aimee, I also have a secret, and it's not so great." She touched the back of her hand to my cheek. The skin of her knuckles wore calluses. "It's not so great at all."

My mother entered. "Is Aimee going on about the secret project already? You haven't even had a moment to rest."

I stuck out my tongue and ran outside to play with Ainara. Since we began working on Father's secret project together, Yen and I had spent more time together without Ainara. She asked every day for a month about the secret project, and every day I came up with new ways of telling her no.

That night, I didn't eat much and couldn't sleep, excited that Eyun had returned and that soon the village would see the magical lantern I'd helped my father build.

I got up in the middle of the night and tiptoed into the darkened kitchen. I felt for the stool I sat on to tend the fire and placed it against the wall. When I stood on the stool, I could reach the first two items on a high shelf: a glass bottle of seasoning powder and a small jar of *La Bai Cai*, spicy preserved Chinese cabbage. I grabbed both, stepped carefully down from the stool, and eased out the front door.

My mother had told us that only female mosquitoes bite because they need the blood to make babies. I thought even mosquitoes needed a future, so after I settled on the stoop, I lifted my sleeves and pant legs for their bites.

I ate, sprinkling a white mound of seasoning powder on my tongue and following it with a bite of cabbage. The moon was almost full in the sky. The last of the ladybugs had departed our western wall hours ago.

Eyun, pale and ghostly in a white shift, came out to join me. She went over to study the caged rabbits, her red hair shining purple in the blue moonlight. When she turned back to me, she smiled in an odd way. "It's easy for them. They have no need for love, and their lives are short."

"Yes, we eat them after a month or two, but there's more of them all the time. Last month six escaped by digging a hole out of their pen and into a neighbor's storage hut down the road. They claimed they never saw any rabbits, but I smelled rabbit stew a few nights later."

"Maybe their lives are not so simple after all." She came to sit beside me, the moon casting long shadows across her face.

"Are you sad because Jian couldn't come with you this time?" I took another mouthful, and spicy cabbage burst on my tongue.

"No, Aimee. Jian's never coming with me again."

I swallowed, and felt the warmth burn down my throat.

"Does he hate the cold that much? It's barely autumn. You can tell him it's not so cold now. Tell him I said so."

She shook her head. "It's not the cold. It's me. He doesn't like me enough."

"Oh." I tried to think of something encouraging to say, but nothing came.

"He's stupid, then. How can he not like you? You're a smart and beautiful scientist."

"I am from a small village in the northeast, and he wanted better."

"But he's from a tent in the southwest. Even smaller than our village."

A corner of Eyun's lip quirked, but it was not a smile. Her eyes fell to the moonlight reflecting off the River of Stories. "And that's why he wants better. Who you choose to spend your life with greatly influences what your life will be. And he chose someone else."

"That's really stupid. You spend your life with yourself first, I think, and then you choose people." I stopped doling out childish wisdom when my aunt started to cry. One tear escaped her altogether and landed on my shoulder. She'd always seemed independent and strong, needing no one but herself. "I'm sorry. Don't listen to me."

"No, it's good advice. I guess in a way Jian chose himself too. Remember I told you he made things that were aerodynamic?"

I nodded.

"And you said 'airplanes' and I said 'something like that'? Aimee, he does not make planes. He makes missiles. When he met a general's daughter, she told him right away she wanted him and he thought that was refreshing and brave. I'd never told him what I felt in words. She also promised him more military contracts, a house in the city—the world."

I paused for a moment, thinking hard. "He makes missiles?"

"Yes, aerodynamic missiles."

"Then how can you two work in the same company? You make laser lights for concerts."

"Not for concerts, Aimee. I told you that because you were young. I make laser guidance systems so the missiles can be dropped precisely."

"You need to find someone better then!"

She laughed, a crackling sound that emerged from deep within. She lifted me onto her knee and messed my hair with both hands.

"Let me tell you about my secret project with Father," I whispered.

"I can't hear you."

"That's because it's a secret, silly." Our cat chose that moment to sidle up and weave herself around our legs.

Eyun smoothed my hair. "At least I know you won't go around telling everyone my secrets."

"I would never tell anyone someone else's secret. Everyone would be upset with me, and no one would ever tell me secrets again. Not a good plan at all."

"No, indeed." Eyun squinted in the darkness, studying me. "Why are you awake?"

"I was hungry. I'm eating *La Bai Cai* and the white stuff that isn't salt that Mother puts in stir-fry."

"You're eating spicy preserved Chinese cabbage with MSG?"

"It sounds a bit odd when you put it that way. But it tastes good." I smiled. "I can feel the flavor all over my tongue, and then when I go to sleep, I have interesting dreams."

Eyun lifted an eyebrow. "You're a strange child, Aimee."

"What did you snack on when you were a girl? I bet it was weird too."

"I didn't snack when I was a girl."

"So that's why you're so thin."

"Something like that. Time to go to sleep, Aimee. Tomorrow's going to be an exciting day. You don't want to sleep in and miss everything."

"What about you?"

"I'll come inside in a few minutes."

As I went back into the house, I heard the distinctive tsk of a match, and a moment later smelled cigarette smoke. Until then, I hadn't known she smoked.

I WAS THE last one to wake up the next morning.

"Get up, Aimee!" My mother stood over me. Then, a few minutes later, "Aimee, this is your second warning." Then, "It's get-up-or-else time!" She pulled the blanket off me.

I shivered and turned to one side, digging my head extra deep into the pillow to keep warm. A second later, she pulled the pillow out from under my head. I groaned. She was always so cheerful in the morning.

I got up, bleary-eyed and disoriented. My father was telling my grandmother his dream. "It was a giant rat with sharp teeth—I kept trying to kill it. I'd stomp on it, then it would go away and show up again, and I'd stomp it again. I didn't sleep well at all."

I'd dreamed of being chased by a giant. "You were stomping me!" I said.

"What? Don't be silly, Aimee. It was a giant rat, huge."

"Don't worry, I dreamed I bit the giant a few times, so it's all right."

My father studied his arms for bitemarks.

My mother and Aunt Eyun folded the blankets into neat rectangles and placed them back into the cabinet.

Eyun said, "You two were made for each other. An adult and a child, both going on nine."

"I'd rather be going on nine than twenty-six and going on alone," my father muttered.

"Father!" I cried. But the damage was done.

Eyun continued folding covers and piling pillows, but she wouldn't meet our eyes.

"Come on, I need your help with the project." I grabbed my father's hand and led him to the root cellar shed. We'd only finished all the pieces of our lantern the day before, and it lay in an organized heap in the corner.

My father lifted parts of the lantern and repositioned them. "What's wrong with your aunt?"

"She's . . . well, just don't talk to her about Jian."

"It was a joke. I figured she and Jian would be married soon."

I thought about saying more, but decided against it. "Just don't make any more jokes about that."

He shook his head with a bemused smile. "Little Aimee, keeper of secrets."

Yen poked his head into the shed. "Is it time to move him?"

We wrapped our lantern in a burlap cloth and tied it with twine. As we walked to the village square where the lantern festival would be held, my father carried the head and body, and Yen and I trailed with the limbs.

THE WHOLE VILLAGE sang in Manchu to open the Moon Festival. My mother's perfect voice joined the wind as if it were a part of the landscape. I was shrill, but my soprano peaks were canceled by Grandfather Feng's baritone valleys. My father, who was born far away in the capital of Beijing, didn't know Manchu, so he hummed along instead.

The other twenty-nine competitors for best lantern set up in their allotted space in numbered order: traditional red balloon lanterns with gold trim, six-sided lanterns with candles inside that drove pinwheels so images danced, cubic lanterns with calligraphy and painting on each side, and other unique creations.

Father's entry was last. When the judge started viewing number one, we were still setting ours up. Father's friends in the village speculated whether this was because he wanted to keep them in suspense until the very last moment.

Entry number eight was a koi fish that moved its tail from side to side and wowed the children.

Entry number fifteen was a goose whose head bounced up and down, pecking at the ground. It looked great for the first few pecks, before the beak dug too deep into the earth and broke.

Entry number twenty-seven was a dragon that breathed fire. Entry number twenty-nine bounced up and down, a buzzing bee suspended from a spring coil on a bamboo pole.

We kept our lantern under a layer of burlap until the last moment. The other lanterns ran on candlelight, but ours ran on fireflies. I had collected them in a jar by singing a Manchu song to lure lightning. Just before the unveiling, I dove under the burlap to release the insects into the body of the lantern.

When the judge called out for entry number thirty, my father and I simultaneously drew back the burlap. There were sniggers in the audience—our figure of a man standing with hands held together was thin and dark.

The judge raised an eyebrow and lifted his pen to write on his pad. "A large construction," he said. "But not much light, considering it's the light competition."

"Aimee, would you do the honors?" my father asked.

I cupped my hands and sang to the fireflies. The man's chest glowed with warmth in response. Fireflies danced inside, lighting then dimming so that the man appeared alive and iridescent. His head looked imperiously at the crowd, bright eyes glowing where we had installed cut marbles. His arms opened. The sniggering was replaced by sounds of awe. Ainara jumped up and down, clapping her hands in joy.

The judge raised his eyebrows. "Which historical figure is this?"

The judge looked at my father and then at me.

I stopped singing. The fireflies gathered in the lantern's hands and a beam of red light like a laser shot out from each hand. One beam found Eyun. The other passed between people in the crowd and continued out of the village. I tugged my father's sleeve.

My father's eyes also found Eyun. A breeze floated her flame-red hair around her face, and he inclined his head as if in apology. "It's Laoyue, the old man of the moon who ties the red ribbon of fate."

My father's lantern won that year.

NINE

The dusty dirt road to our village was now paved, and many of the trees on either side had transformed into houses. Chrome toll booths marked the border where stretches of highway built by one construction company butted up against sections built by another.

I had called my sister again from the hotel in Harbin but got only a busy signal. I wondered what my family would say when they saw me and David, the worries in me both anchor and lodestone.

We passed a lime-green sign on the side of the road that was in both Chinese and Manchu. Eternal Spring, Population 200,000.

I gasped. "Two hundred thousand?"

David whistled. "That's not a village."

"It was. It is. It was only 900 when I was a child."

"The oil boom must have really boomed."

The bus jostled over a canary-yellow speed bump and I bounced in my seat. "Grandfather Feng always said there was lots of oil here. He said we sat in a giant concave wok. Since there was oil in the nearby towns, on the edges of the wok, that meant Eternal Spring was at its depth, the richest deposit of all."

"Smart man."

"He was right about a lot of things. Crazy, but right." We pulled up to a shiny new terminal.

The other passengers pressed past us, keen to get off the bus. On the ground, the bus driver handed David his luggage last, then gave me a map. "First time in Eternal Spring?"

"No, but it's been a long time. Everything's so different."

He pointed at the pink concrete slabs stretching away from the terminal to the adjacent public square. "That's the People's Square. You'll find a taxi stand there."

When I just blinked, he chuckled, then pointed. "Ice Dragon Mountain is that way, the River of Stories is over there."

I thanked him, and he said, "*Bu yong xie.*" No need to thank.

I checked my watch: 12:01 p.m. "I think we can walk from here. Our house wasn't far from the farmer's market, which used to be here."

As we walked, twelve-foot-tall stone statues of famous historical figures cast tight, dark shadows in our path. The Nishan shaman was among them. And the woman who founded our village of Eternal Spring. One depicted a fierce Manchu warrior with his longbow drawn, surveying the landscape. "Nurhaci," I explained. "The man who united the Manchu tribes and then conquered all of China."

"Yep, that's what it says."

I glanced at the plaque and was surprised to find the text in Chinese and English.

The roads had been broadened and paved, and were filled with a crush of people and cars I couldn't have imagined in my childhood. All of it was in soft focus. The colors of jacket sleeves blended into car bumpers. There were no edges.

Jet lag.

The map had the larger streets and avenues written in both Manchu and Chinese. As we walked, I squinted, only able to recognize a few of the names. Where the translator took poetic liberties or new streets had been built, I had no hope of deciphering the secrets.

I tried to find my childhood home by counting footsteps, painfully aware that my stride was longer than when I was a girl. Was there a conversion available between a child's skipping step and an adult's cautious one?

David, still hanging on to my hand, said, "Are you sure you can find the way?"

"I'm sure." I wanted to find my home by memory alone. To prove to myself that I was from this place and still belonged here. I put the map in my purse.

We walked three blocks in one direction, then I turned us back around. The sun followed us with that peculiar rose tint that colored my every memory of Eternal Spring. At least that was familiar.

I'd not only miscalculated the number of footsteps, but I'd also misremembered the distance. By some magic these things canceled each other out. We now stood at the intersection nearest my childhood home, the dirt path now a street with two lanes in each direction, streetlights swinging above it like ceremonial lanterns.

I checked my watch: 12:15 p.m.

An old man shuffled past us, carrying a grocery bag.

"Excuse me, is this Qian An Street?" I asked.

He gestured and his sleeve vibrated in the breeze. "Oh yes. Well, it was. It hasn't been called that for a long time now. Now it's Convenience Drive."

"Thank you, old teacher."

"Don't be so polite." He stared at David a long moment, then nodded at me and continued down the street. We crossed the road, and I saw with horror why the street name had changed: there sat a convenience store that stretched the length of what had been our house and Yen's house together. A hair salon was next to it, then a fast food place called McChinese. Bile climbed my throat.

I pointed at the intersection. "My grandmother and her friends used to play chess right here. Under an old weeping willow that gave beautiful dappled shade."

David's hand came to rest on the curve of my back. "But you know your family moved. I remember you telling me when they did."

I looked at him with alarm. *My family doesn't live here anymore. They haven't lived here for years.* "I . . . When I thought of home, I thought of where I grew up." My mouth felt dry. I coughed and realized the same amount of dust still floated in the air, though now it tasted of diesel and tar.

I sighed, and we walked toward the convenience store. I needed to soothe my parched throat before I could face talking to my family. I would be returning home to an address that I had only ever seen on envelopes.

The shelves groaned with the things that exist in all convenience stores: junk food, magazines, colorful bottles of sugar-spiked liquid. I took two bottles of water from the fridge and went to the cash.

I pointed to a corner of the store. "My father once scrubbed the coating from the inside of long fluorescent light tubes and filled them with electric eels. They'd light up at night, right about in that spot. It was beautiful." At least, that's what I meant to say. I couldn't think of the Chinese word for fluorescent and ended up telling the clerk that my father had kept eels inside electric light bulbs.

I handed him the money and frowned when he didn't say "Thank you." The Chinese don't spend all day thanking each other for nothing. It's a cultural thing I'd forgotten.

He waved at David and said "Hello" in English. When David said hello back, the man said hello again. It was the only English word he knew.

"*Ni hao*," David tried in Chinese, which unleashed a torrent of Chinese from the man. David spread his palms upward and shrugged, and we left the store.

On the street, I bumped into a person shorter and softer than me.

"*Dui bu qi*." Sorry.

The man turned. He was of that indefinable age when the lines are etched so long in permanent frown or permanent laugh that he could have been seventy or a hundred. His eyes were bright and wild, his hair white and standing on end. He sang a song about crickets and ladybugs. Then he said, "It's difficult to see the world for what it is when you don't look."

A cricket chirped nearby.

I squinted at him. "Do I know you?"

"What a silly question. How can I know if you know me? I can only know if I know you, maybe."

"*Do* you know me? I am Wu Aimee, previously of Qian An Street."

"*Aiyah*!" He laughed hysterically, pulling on tufts of hair at his temples. "Aimee. Yes, yes, I do know if you know me!"

"Grandfather Feng!"

He nodded, his head bobbing like a frozen persimmon floating in water. "Feng de Feng," he said. The Mad Feng. "Aimee, it's been months since you came back from high school for summer break. Everyone will be so happy, everyone, your Yen and your Ainara, your father and your mother—"

How could he not know? "I'm sorry, Grandfather Feng. I have a letter from Ainara that says our mother died."

"Your problem," he lectured, one finger pointed toward the tip of my nose, "is you're a bird flying high while the dew is still upon the grass."

Maybe the letter was wrong. Maybe the translator had made a mistake. "But my mother *is* dead. Isn't she?"

"There is a hundred percent chance she is alive. And there is a hundred percent chance she is dead."

Perhaps the translator was wrong. Perhaps—

Feng grabbed my hand and led me up the street. David hung on to my other hand. I translated for him rapidly but couldn't keep up with Feng's flow of words.

"I will tell you a joke. You and Yen are in the mountains hunting for ginseng. You see one next to a stream and run forward, and Yen follows. All of a sudden, you both stop because a bear rises up on its rear legs in front of you and it's howling mad. Yen stays frozen, pretends to be dead. You stretch your arms and warm up your legs.

"Yen says, 'What do you think you're doing? You can't outrun the bear.'

"And you say, 'I don't have to outrun the bear. I only have to outrun you!'"

Feng laughed too loud, and for too long.

"Grandfather Feng, I don't think that's funny."

He stopped so quickly David bumped into me. "What troubles do you have in your heart, Aimee? Speak them out loud, so the rest of us can have a good laugh!" He laughed even louder, then dragged us skipping through the street as he sang a song about a girl with hair made of eels.

Feng's steps were sure and rhythmic. He jumped over pebbles and leaped cracks in the pavement.

Fear and joy and pain swirled inside me. He led us left, then right, then stopped, squinted and pounded his fist at the wooden door of an immaculate red brick house.

He let go of my hand.

My heart drummed so hard I could feel the rhythm in my ears.

A perfect stranger opened the door. She was about thirty—tall and so slender the wind might blow her away just by thinking. Her hair was dyed chestnut, and she wore pink cotton slippers. "May I help you?"

I flipped through the faces in my memory for who she could possibly be. She wasn't Ainara. She wasn't one of my cousins. Yes, years had gone by, but I didn't recognize her.

I cleared my throat and tried to speak, but found my voice too thick with emotion. I tried again. "I'm Wu Aimee."

She looked from me to David and back again. "I'm not buying whatever it is you're selling." She slammed the door and locked it.

My face drained of blood and I turned to David. "I have no idea who she was."

For once, my husband had no soothing words.

Feng was gone as if he had never been there. Disoriented, I looked around and saw we had returned to Convenience Drive. Feng had led us in a circle.

When it was called Qian An Street, our house was the last one at the west end of the road, next to the River of Stories. But Convenience Drive had grown as the village grew. We stood in front of a house just to the east of the convenience store.

I stood on the edge of lost time.

WE TRACED OUR steps back to People's Square and took a taxi to the address on my sister's letter. I fingered the edge of the envelope in my purse and looked out the window. I tried to remember Eternal Spring as the village it once was, but its mud-brick and wood buildings had been replaced by steel and concrete; hand-sewn navy pants and jackets had given way to blue jeans and pink lace shirts. Hair salons stood on every block.

If the village had changed so much, surely my family had also. Since my mother and I became estranged, I'd written less often to my sister and father too. I called only on Chinese New Year, when there was room for few meaningful words between greetings and well wishes, with fireworks in the background.

"It's strange, going home to a house I've never been to," I said.

"It's not the house, it's the people."

I was grateful for the solidity of David's presence. I'd lived eighteen years before we met, but it was difficult to imagine a time when he was not in my life. I smiled at him.

"I hope your family likes me," he said, looking nervous.

I spoke with more assurance than I felt. "They're going to love you."

We arrived at a two-story red brick house with white framed windows and a door wrapped in steel. The window boxes burst with orange and red flowers, a last hurrah before winter. I took a deep breath as I got out of the taxi, and the air smelled for a moment as I remembered it: earth moist from autumn rains, grass and chrysanthemums.

David said, "It'll be all right." One thing I knew about my husband—he only told me things were going to be all right at the most dire moments.

Boom. Boom. Boom.

I knocked three times, my knuckles smarting from the metal. I waited, pulse throbbing at a point between my eyes. No one answered. When I lifted my hand to knock again, David pointed to a glowing white button on the door frame. Feeling foolish, I pressed the doorbell.

The sound echoed inside the house, an untuned electric guitar. Footsteps approached. I squared my shoulders and forced myself to lift my chin. So many years away, and now I was returning with no advance warning.

A tall, lanky man with kind eyes opened the door. He was taller and more muscular than the last time I'd seen him ten years ago—he'd held hands with Ainara when they all bid me goodbye.

He tilted his head and squinted at me for two long seconds. "Aimee! I hardly recognize you." He flashed a smile, then looked from me to David and back again. "Come in, come in."

I said, in Chinese, "This is my husband, David." And then, in English, "This is my sister's husband, Yen."

They shook hands. David said "*Ni hao*," and Yen said "Hello," both of them sounding strange speaking the other's language.

We stepped into the entryway and Yen gestured for David to drop his suitcase.

I touched Yen's hand, happy for proof I'd made it home. "It's been so long."

He looked shocked at the contact, but recovered fast. "I wish it was under better circumstances, but I'm glad you're home."

He ushered us into the living room. A calligraphy painting of ginseng plants morphing into galloping horses stretched the length of the wall above the sofa. My father and my sister sat at the dining table playing chess as my grandmother looked on. It was the same hardwood table from my childhood, the surface lined and pitted from years of use. My father's arm hovered above the board about to make his next move against Ainara, but I had no doubt that my grandmother advised them both.

My grandmother was so dedicated to her course of herbs and *taiji* that she looked as ageless as when I'd last seen her.

My sister was now a woman of twenty-seven who looked startlingly similar to the way our mother had looked when I was a child. She was thick around the waist with a pregnancy she hadn't told me about. We had been close, once, Ainara and I.

My father glanced at me, his brows drawn together and his lips thinned to a blade. He dropped his arm and chess pieces clattered to the porcelain floor in slow motion. If I'd had my Nikon camera, I would have captured their fall.

A little girl I hadn't noticed scampered under the table, picking up pawns and rooks and passing them up to the adults. A Tamagotchi bracelet on her wrist beeped when she stood up and she pressed buttons on its face.

"Look who's back," Ainara said. "Lien, say hello to your auntie Aimee."

The girl waved at me. "Hello, Auntie Aimee." Her cheeks dimpled when she smiled.

Ainara got up, picked up teacups from the table and walked into the kitchen.

I stood in the middle of the room, unsure if I should come any closer uninvited. Yen loitered near the entryway. David came and stood next to me.

"Aimee." My grandmother lined up the chess pieces. After she completed a row, she looked up at me. "You've aged." She softened it with a smile.

"I have."

"We've all aged. Not your mother, though—she's done with that now." She didn't sound sad, which seemed strange to me.

"She's in heaven with the angels and Buddhas!" Lien shouted as she scrabbled across the floor, hunting for more dropped chess pieces. The Tamagotchi on her wrist chirped.

"Father." I took a step forward.

My father didn't turn to me. He spoke to Lien instead. "That's right," he said. "Our chess game's over, so why don't you and I go play something else? Let's look at our calendars and see what we're supposed to be studying today, hm?"

Lien nodded and took my father's hand, waving at us as they disappeared down a hallway, her wrist beeping into silence.

I bit my lower lip and fought tears.

No one had asked us to sit, so I told myself that after the plane and train and bus and taxi, I was glad to be standing.

Ainara came back with a wooden box she handed to my grandmother, who stacked the chess pieces inside it. "How long are you going to stay?" Ainara asked.

I shook my head. We should be talking about something else. My mother's funeral, for example. Had I missed it all? What had become of her?

Ainara repeated the question, an edge to her voice I'd never heard before.

I looked from her to my grandmother, seeing the similar way they frowned, the angle of their heads so different from mine. I babbled. "I could only get a few days off work, plus the weekends, and another two more if I call in sick. But there's the twelve-hour time difference, and our flight from Beijing to Harbin was canceled, so we had to take a train. I used up three days just getting here. I can only stay a week."

"It's been ten years and you can only stay seven days," Ainara said.

I focused on a junction of porcelain tiles on the floor, sure that shame was clear on my face. "I need—we need—three days for the return trip."

Yen stepped forward, his hands up in peace. "Seven days is better than none."

"I came as soon as I received the letter. I tried to call, but my calls didn't go through." I looked down, couldn't tell them I had to get the letter translated. I looked up. "I hoped I'd make it in time for the funeral."

My grandmother, Ainara and Yen all froze.

"Did I get here on time?"

My grandmother frowned. "Funeral?"

I nodded, straightening my back. I was a bad daughter who was away when my mother died, but I was here now.

Ainara came to me then, standing so close she blocked my view of my grandmother. "It's against the law to bury anybody. There's too many people and not enough earth."

I didn't understand.

"The hospital cremated her the day she died. There was no funeral."

I reached for her, but Ainara stepped back and my hands closed on nothing.

In all my calculations of days and hours, of steps and distance, of coming home as soon as possible, it had never occurred to me there wouldn't *be* a funeral to miss.

The white queen, who had been lying on her side, rolled off the table and hit the floor with the force of a grenade.

It was the middle of the day. Or the middle of the night. Or the middle of nothing at all. My world flashed black, the edges nonexistent. My limbs shook as if I'd been hit by lightning.

I slipped from David's grip, knees hitting the porcelain tiles.

I was blind.

TEN

In Chinese, Monday is *Xing qi yi*, "week day one," Tuesday is *Xing qi er*, "week day two," and so on. Sunday, though, is not week day seven but day *tian*. *Tian* is a word with two meanings. It is "sky" as much as it is "heaven." Thus, Sunday was day heaven.

Our father left at dawn with a few sheets of paper and a fine-tipped paintbrush tucked into his jacket pocket. "Wait for me. I will be back at noon. At 12:33, something amazing is going to happen." Ainara and I nodded and smiled.

My mother grabbed us by our wrists. "Come help."

The three of us spent the rest of the morning sweeping the floor, washing clothes and polishing enamel bowls and dishes.

Slanting morning light from our single kitchen window highlighted the lines around her eyes. I saw in her a glimmer of age. One day, she would be old. There had been a day when she was as young as I was then. There would be a day when I was older than my mother at that moment.

Ainara held up her enamel bowl to inspect it in the light from the window. "I enjoy cleaning. Everything finishes so neat and tidy."

I shook my head. "I don't."

"You don't?" My mother sounded surprised.

"There are so many better things to do."

"Cleaning is wonderful," my sister insisted.

"I want to grow up, so I never have to clean again."

My mother chuckled. "What will you do when you grow up instead of clean?"

"I will be an artist."

Ainara puffed her cheeks and whistled out a breath. "Artists starve."

"If all artists starve, then how can they get married and have children who become more artists?"

My mother shook her head. "Artists are not born."

"Yes, they are. Father's an artist and so I'm an artist too."

Ainara polished her already shiny bowl absently. "But Mother likes cleaning, and you hate cleaning."

"That's different. Art is special; cleaning isn't."

Ainara set the bowl down. "Either you can be born something or you can't. If you can be born an artist, then you can be born a clean person."

My mother patted us each on the head. The lines of her lightning scar moved on her wrist as if alive. "I'm so tired." She sat on a kitchen stool, laid her head on the counter, and fell asleep.

I squinted at the bright sunlight outside and thought how odd it was she'd fallen asleep in the middle of the morning. "Mother," I whispered. "Mother, are you really asleep?"

When I asked her this at night, lying next to her on the *kang* bed, she would whisper back, "Of course I'm asleep, Aimee. You should be too. I will see you in my dreams."

This time she didn't answer.

Ainara shrugged and moved on to polishing a porcelain teapot whose surface already shone.

I folded up the towel I was using and laid it on the counter.

Cleaning was endless. No matter how many times we scrubbed the wok or polished the enamelware bowls, they would only get dirty again. No matter how many times I swept the floor, I couldn't help but think that it was an earthen floor. The floor itself was made of dirt!

Glancing at my sleeping mother one more time, I decided it would be better to fetch my grandmother than to carry on cleaning. I skipped down the road to find my grandmother sitting with several friends at a round stone table that served as a chessboard. Before I was born, my father had carved bones for the white pieces and walnut wood for the black.

Yen's mother sat on one side of the board and another neighbor, Mr. Yu, sat on the other. The onlookers—my grandmother and two older men—talked about the game from behind cupped hands. Yen's mother rubbed her jaw then looked at my grandmother, who leaned in and pointed. "If it were me playing, I would suggest moving this to here."

Yen's mother did as she suggested and silence fell over the group. After two more moves, Mr. Yu also looked to my grandmother. She pointed again. "I could suggest moving that to there."

In this way, my grandmother played chess with herself.

I tugged on her arm and whispered, "Mother fell asleep with her head on the kitchen counter."

She turned and stared at me, then got up and hurried back to the house with me on her heels.

MY MOTHER WAS still slumped over the kitchen counter and Ainara was still polishing the same teapot. My grandmother took Mother's pulse, two fingers placed on the pressure points at her wrist.

"Get my medical bag."

I rushed into the living room, but Ainara beat me to it. We each grabbed a handle and delivered the heavy leather bag together, faster but clumsier than we would have been on our own. Grandmother opened it and withdrew a glass bottle, a cotton ball and a tiny paper envelope.

"What's the diagnosis, doctor?" I said, parroting the neighbors she saw on her rounds.

"It's her *xin*, her heart. She has a small *xin* and it has a small hole in it." She meant it literally, but I thought she was speaking metaphorically. Small heart—*xiao xin*—meant to be careful.

Ainara must have thought the same, because she said, "Mother is always careful with everything she does. What do you mean she has a small hole?"

My grandmother soaked the cotton ball in the liquid from the bottle. "Your mother was born with a tiny hole in her heart. It leaks blood. Not much," she said, noticing how worried we looked, "but enough that sometimes when she works too hard or pushes herself too much or *cao xin*, worries too much, she becomes faint."

Ainara frowned. "How tiny a hole?"

"The size of the black dot on the back of a ladybug."

I chewed my lower lip. "Mother says each of those dots is a story."

My grandmother nodded. She removed an acupuncture needle from its envelope and inserted it into the tip of my mother's thumb, twisting as it sunk deeper. She stroked my mother's hair and rubbed her ears to bring her soul back to her body.

"Come back, daughter. Come back from wherever it is you have wandered alone and we cannot follow."

My eyes met Ainara's. Our mother had gone where we could not follow. But I would follow her anywhere. She was my mother and I was her daughter. If she was not here, and I was not her daughter, then what was I?

Ainara's crinkled expression mirrored my own. I held her hand, not sure if I was offering support or taking it.

My grandmother looked zen, yet I knew she was being calm for our sake. I decided to be calm for her and Ainara and not cry.

I stroked the warm pulse at my mother's neck, "Come back to me. Come now, come quickly. I promise to clean happily." *I still want to be an artist, but I can be an artist who cleans.*

My grandmother said, "In Traditional Chinese Medicine, we say anything that happens too quickly is never good."

My mother's pulse thudded and restarted at a higher pace. It beat with promises of love, of time, of eternity.

She blinked. "I must have nodded off. I've been so tired lately."

Ainara hugged her around the waist.

My grandmother gave my mother a severe look and said, "Lie down and rest now."

"Lying down is for the sick and the dead. To prove to my body I'm well, I need to keep moving." Our mother shed her apron and began putting a lacquerware bowl on its shelf.

If she recovered so fast, then the tiny hole in her heart must not be a big problem, I thought.

FATHER RETURNED AT noon as promised. He had traded paper-and-ink drawings he'd made on scraps of paper for two stiff pieces of cardboard. One piece was as large as my chest. The other fit into his hand and had a tiny hole in the center.

I thought of the hole in Mother's heart.

Ainara ran to him. "Mother has a hole in her heart, and she fell asleep."

He looked less worried than I expected. "But she's fine now?"

I nodded.

"Look, Aimee." He held up the two pieces of cardboard. "I've got you your first camera."

I laughed, because I knew a camera was more than two pieces of paper.

Ainara laughed too. "That's not a camera. A camera is what a photographer has in a studio."

"No, seriously. This is a camera." He pointed to the sky.

Ainara glanced up and gasped. "The sun is not round!"

Strange. I thought the sun was always round. It was a shock to find I was wrong.

"Don't stare at it—you'll hurt your eyes." My father laid the larger cardboard sheet on the ground in the center of the yard, and handed me the smaller piece. "Hold it horizontal, so the sun shines through the hole and the light lands on the other sheet."

I did as he instructed. On the sheet of cardboard on the ground, an image of the sun appeared.

"Someone's eating the sun in bites," I said.

"I want to try too!" Ainara grabbed at the small piece of cardboard, but I held it above her head.

I told her a story Mother had told me the week before. "In Ice Dragon Mountain lived a fox and two pigs. The pigs cooked a pie and argued about how to divide it equally. Since they didn't trust each other, they asked the fox to help them. The fox broke the pie into two pieces."

"I don't know this story."

"One pig said, 'His piece is bigger than mine!' So the fox took a bite out of the larger one.

"Then the other pig said, 'But now his piece is bigger!' So the fox took a bite out of that one."

Ainara clapped in delight.

"And so it continued until the fox had eaten the entire pie. The pigs complained, and the fox said, 'That was a nice appetizer, but I'm still hungry,' and ate both pigs."

Ainara pointed at me, laughing. "That's a wonderful and terrible story."

I looked up at the sun, then down at the image on the big piece of cardboard—the sun, down on the ground. One bite at a time, the fox was eating the sun.

I moved my finger over the tiny hole and the image of the sun disappeared. I moved my finger out of the way, and it reappeared. I lifted the small card to my eye and looked at the sun through the tiny hole. Then I handed the cardboard to Ainara, and she did the same, frowning.

All the while, as we were trying to puzzle out a solution, our father smiled.

Ainara flipped the cardboard and checked the other side. "What's the trick? How do you make the sun look not round?"

Father chuckled. "There's no trick. The sun is being eclipsed by the moon, which happens every time the moon travels in front of the sun."

I frowned. "But the moon is much smaller than the sun. How does the moon block something so much bigger?"

"Even though the sun is bigger, it's farther away. When objects are closer to you, they seem larger. See Yen." My father pointed. Yen was coming out of his house with something clasped in one hand. "He's closer to you, and that's why he seems much larger than the people playing chess down the street. He can block your view by being close to you."

I waved. "Yen! Come over so you can be larger for me."

"What do you have in your hand?" Ainara reached out, a blush lighting her cheeks when their fingertips touched.

Yen revealed a glass oval that was probably once the lens from a pair of glasses, but now was darkened by oil or smoke. Ainara held it up and peered through it, then handed it to me.

I moved to clean it on my shirt hem, but Yen stopped me. "No, I made it that way on purpose. I can't touch the stars if I can't see them, and the sun is a star."

I handed him the glass and returned to fiddling with the small piece of cardboard while Yen and Ainara played together, passing the smoked glass back and forth and peering through it at each other.

Finally, my father was ready to explain. "The hole in the smaller cardboard creates what is called a 'pinhole camera' effect, focusing the image from the sun. It reverses it, then projects it onto the cardboard on the ground."

I rolled the new words on my tongue. "Pinhole camera. But I can't take a photo with it, can I? I won't have a photo for afterward."

"That's true, you can't keep what you see. But it is a camera nonetheless."

"But what's the point if it won't last?"

My father laughed. "If you had photo paper and built a box around the sheet on the ground, you could create a physical photograph. But, Aimee, nothing lasts. Even when you take a photo and print it, it will turn yellow and brittle over time. One day it will be dust."

It didn't seem meaningful to have something that didn't last. I wanted to take a photo that would last forever.

My mother came toward us, her footfalls precise. "Look, Mother, I'm so bright I made the sun come to earth with a piece of cardboard."

My mother patted me on the head. "You *are* very bright."

The sun was now two-thirds eaten, and my mother's shadow drew out longer and longer. The sky was dark like evening, yet the shadows were highly contrasted, as if in the face of competing darkness, they had reached even greater depth.

"Let me show you how it works." As I clasped my mother's hand, my thumb brushed the spot where my grandmother had inserted her acupuncture needle. I shivered and released her. I gave her the smaller cardboard and pointed to the ground where the larger one lay, explaining what to do.

She looked down. "It's so small, the image on the ground. When I was a girl, we used to look at an eclipse directly through a smoked glass."

Yen smiled and held up his dirty oval, as Ainara beamed at him. He turned his face toward the sun, holding a hand over one eye and the darkened piece of glass over the other.

"Yen, the smoked glass doesn't protect your eyes completely," my father warned. "You shouldn't look at the sun because it will burn you."

Ainara tilted her head. "But the sun is less bright during an eclipse."

"No, it's not. When you look at the sun on a normal day, the irises of your eyes contract to protect you. During a total eclipse, the sun is still as bright, but your eyes are fooled, and your irises expand. You can look directly only when the eclipse is total."

I frowned in concentration. "So, to see it, you have to not see it."

My father nodded.

I looked up. The sun was a black center surrounded by a circle of light. Solar flares peeked through the valleys of the moon, casting all the colors with names and many without. Yen stood between Ainara and me, close enough that his proximity would block the light of many things if I allowed it.

I took a mental photo. I tried to remember him exactly as he was at that moment, his face angled to the sun, enveloped in darkness and light.

ELEVEN

I woke up struggling. David caught me and pulled me to his chest. "Morning," he whispered. I was so grateful he didn't say, "Good morning."

Last night, after I collapsed, they had carried me here to Lien's bed. I barely fit, which meant David's feet hung over the end. A clock ticked near my head on the bedside table. Touching it told me it was rabbit-shaped, but didn't tell me the time. I asked David.

"It's 7:12 a.m. How are your eyes?"

The world was the same black with them open or closed. I left them open, as if that would make a difference. "I still can't see. Also, I have no clean clothes. What will I wear?"

"We need to get you to a doctor."

"There are two doctors in this house," I said.

David ignored me and continued. "We'll find you the best eye doctor when we're back home and I'm sure we'll get this resolved quickly. And you do have clothes. You can wear mine." The mattress flexed as David leaned away then he pressed the fabric of a football jersey into my hands. On lazy Sundays in New York, I'd wear his Chicago Bears jersey all day.

When I didn't move, he lifted my arms over my head and guided me into the shirt.

"Thank you."

"No need to thank," he said.

I appreciated his effort to make me smile, even if it didn't work. "You should say it in Chinese. *Bu yong xie.*"

"Boo yun say."

"*Bu yong xie.*"

"Boo ung xie."

"Close enough."

Outside our room, slippers pattered on tile and chopsticks clinked against dishes. "Are they having breakfast?"

"I think so."

That hurt me. We'd always eaten together as a family. But of course, it had been a long time since I was a part of this family. "I wish they'd woken us."

"You collapsed, Amy. They likely wanted you to rest."

"Maybe," I murmured.

David helped me find my way into a pair of his pants, rolling up the legs and belting the waist. I felt like a child again. I despaired, but crying would not have made my mother proud. I ran my fingers through my tangles. "At least I can't see that it's a mess."

"I love it when your hair's a mess. But your family might not agree." He placed the brush in my hand. "You're bad at asking for help."

"I'm not." I rubbed the ache in my neck where I had slept on it at the wrong angle.

"You are. Being strong doesn't mean doing everything by yourself. You can ask for help from the people who love you. You don't refuse it when it's given, but you don't ask for it when you need it."

"I don't want to be a burden."

"Amy, we do things for each other. That's what relationships are."

"You're only saying that because I'm blind."

I heard him take a breath, then sigh it out. "I try to give you what you want, but maybe I don't give you what you need."

I needed not to be blind. I needed to reconcile with my dead mother. No one could give me that. "What do you think I need?"

"To be challenged."

I actually cackled. "I'm blind. I think that's challenge enough." I enunciated every word, as if speaking a foreign language. "I am a blind *photographer*."

"Beethoven was a deaf composer. He wrote music in his mind, and by feeling the vibrations of the piano."

"You're comparing me to Beethoven?"

"I'm just saying that you'll learn to use your other senses."

"So you think this is permanent."

"I don't know, Amy. Only the doctors can tell us."

I fell silent, considering David's particular brand of optimism. "So I'll learn to detect my subjects by their sounds and compose images by feel?"

"Maybe. Or locate them by smell and arrange them by taste." He paused for a laugh that didn't come. "I should've pushed you to talk with your mother. You're such an independent woman that I—"

I bristled. "Is that a problem?"

"No, I love that about you. But we've been married six years, and sometimes you still strike me like someone who appeared in the world one day completely formed."

I frowned. "That's because you didn't know I came from this place. Maybe I . . . also didn't know."

A long silence stretched between us. When we were new to each other, before he had a company that required all-nighters and before I became addicted to stalking strangers through the streets with my camera, we would lie in bed and do nothing but talk. It was the most intimate thing in the world.

"I was surprised you came with me. I'd never ask you to choose between me and your work."

"The sun's been around for 4.6 billion years. It can wait another few days."

"Science humor."

"Now, you really do need me." He leaned in, and I felt his warm breath on my forehead. I closed my eyes and he kissed each eyelid. "I'll be your seeing-eye human. I'll help you cross the street."

I went to swat him but missed. "Will you guide me to my family?" When he didn't respond, I said, "You're nodding, aren't you?"

He laughed. "Yes, I am." David placed my hand on the crook of his arm and led me from the room.

I heard Lien's Tamagotchi beep repeatedly, then her

voice complaining. "Brown's so boring. I want color! I want to wear my panda dress with the pink shoes."

Ainara sounded exasperated. "The pink shoes don't fit you anymore, and they clash with the panda print. In my day, we would've been happy to have brown leather shoes."

"But you're old, Mom, and I know it was tough for you. In tribute to your suffering, let me wear the pink shoes. Please?"

Ainara huffed. "Wear whatever you want. If those shoes give you blisters, don't complain to me."

The hardwood underfoot transitioned to the cold porcelain tile of the living-dining room. I withdrew my hand from David as wooden chopsticks stilled against ceramic dishes. Ainara's voice carried from across the room. "What are you wearing? You could swim in it. Or drown in it."

"I've no choice. The airline lost my luggage and I have no clothes," I said to Ainara, then translated for David, who said, "You look fine."

"You have clothes here."

Surely my sister hadn't kept my clothes from when I was a teenager. Even if she had, there's no way they would fit me now. "No, I don't."

"Mother sewed new clothes for you."

Heat rose in my cheeks. "When?"

"Always. She sewed clothes for when you'd come back after college. Then she sewed a wedding dress for when you'd come back to get married. After you got married in America, she sewed clothes for when you'd come home again."

Old habits live. It turned out that in the ten years I'd been gone, my mother had sewed forty sets of tops and bottoms, two for every summer and every winter, just like when I was a child. I translated for David. It was even harder repeating it in English than hearing it from Ainara.

"That's sad," he said.

"What did he say?" Ainara asked.

I despaired that they couldn't talk except through me. But of course, my mother and I spoke the same language, and we still didn't understand each other.

I'd been hugging myself, clasping my elbows. My sister's hands pried apart my arms and dropped a heavy weight into them.

I dipped my face, and my cheek landed on soft cotton. I inhaled deeply, hoping to catch the smell of my mother's earthy, sun-warmed hands. Instead, I got a whiff of laundry soap, violets growing in pavement cracks.

"They don't smell bad," Ainara said. "She washed them every year on your birthday and kept them packed in plastic in between."

Her words slapped across my mind. "No—I was hoping they'd smell like her."

"Your sister is crying," David whispered to me.

Ainara's voice sounded distorted, as if it came from underwater. Soft fingertips touched my temple and I startled. "Let me check your eyes," Ainara said.

David guided me to sit on a chair at the dining table, and Ainara examined me. I heard a click. "Follow the light with your eyes," Ainara said.

I could see no light.

"What's wrong with Aunt Aimee?" Lien asked.

Yen cleared his throat as if buying time to consider his

words. "Don't worry. She just has trouble seeing right now. People can go blind from strong emotions. When we were young, it happened to your *nai nai*, and your *lao lao* helped her see again." *Nai nai* was Yen's mother, and *lao lao* was my mother.

I smiled vaguely and said to Yen, "I remember you came over to ask for eye medicine, and Mother gave you athlete's foot cream instead because she had memorized the eye chart to pass her exam. She couldn't read the fine print on the packaging." As the words passed my lips, I realized I was saying a secret out loud, but since Yen's mother had been cured, and my mother was dead now, the secret no longer mattered.

Ainara's fingers poked and prodded around my eyes, circling the problem. "That's not how it happened. I was the one who gave Yen the medicine, and it was eye medicine. After all, his mother used it and could see again. Our mother always wore glasses."

Her explanation sounded rational, but it was not what I remembered. It was such a strange and magical story from our childhood that I had no doubt I remembered it correctly. "Not always," I whispered. "There was a first time. She got glasses after I confronted her about giving Yen the wrong medicine."

"My mother put foot cream on her eyes?" Yen asked.

My father said, "I don't remember this happening. Your mother always wore glasses."

Inside my blindness, I felt like I was going mad. Their voices were sincere, so I knew they weren't teasing me, but I didn't understand how their reality was not the same as mine.

My grandmother chuckled. "The important thing is that Yen's mother recovered and can see."

LIEN AND AINARA left first, one to school and the other to the hospital, on the last workday before the three-day Moon Festival holiday. Yen and my father went off together. Yen worked in the town development office that approved new buildings. My father worked at the office next door, mapping out the roads that were turning Eternal Spring into a city. They were both a vital part of the transformation that had made my home unrecognizable to me.

I wanted to tell them not to go—that I was only home for a few days and they should stay and talk to me, deal with the reality of me. But of course, I couldn't do that.

David excused himself to sleep off the jet lag.

I remained at the dining table, caressing the edge I'd dented with a toy when I was five. I wanted to go to my mother's grave, but there was none.

I wanted to explore the house my family lived in now, see the colors they'd chosen for the walls and read the books on the shelves. I wanted to stare at a photo of my mother. To fall into a photo of my mother. I wanted so much that was impossible.

"How are you doing?" my grandmother said. She'd been so quiet I hadn't realized she was still there.

"I've been better."

She sat beside me and patted my hand, two fingertips

on my pulse. "Blindness forces you to see things you wouldn't otherwise."

I turned my face toward her voice. "I don't see anything at all. All I wanted was to get home in time for Mother's funeral. To find some sort of closure with her. And I've failed."

My grandmother's voice was gentle as her fingers rhythmically stroked my pulse. "You haven't failed. You only fail when you give up."

How was she so zen? I had lost a mother, but she had lost a child.

I shook my head and frowned at the ache in my neck. "How did you say goodbye, when there was no funeral?"

My grandmother's fingers stilled. "That doesn't mean there's no way to say goodbye. Once your mother died, what happened next made no difference to her." She paused as if to carefully choose her words. "The day after your mother died, a lot of the village came to visit, the people who lived here before the oil boom. We scattered her ashes in the river with everyone present."

Everyone.

"Parents shouldn't outlive their children—it's why time works the way it does," my grandmother said. "But from the moment she was born with a tiny hole in her heart, I knew your mother would die young."

I opened my mouth to ask a question, but my grandmother, who was still holding my hand, said, "Here, let me check you." She concentrated again on the two fingers she'd laid on the pulse beating at my wrist. I held my breath.

"Breathe!"

"What's the diagnosis, doctor?"

"Shush." She pulled my other hand toward her.

I was embraced by the scent of roses wafting up from her hair, the lemon starch of her shirt. Two fingers moved along my other wrist, pressing then releasing, pressing then releasing.

I tried for humor. "My heart's okay. There's no hole in it."

"You are so smart, but you never learned. It's not just your outgoing heartbeat I check. It is both the leaving and the returning. We find the nature of what's wrong in the difference between them."

I knew what the difference was. Before the leaving, we were a family. In the returning, my mother was dead and I was a stranger. "Don't you want to check my eyes?"

"The body is a whole system. I check to see your imbalance."

"What if I have no imbalance?"

She laughed. "You're blind, Aimee."

I nodded, pursing my lips.

"If you don't stop pouting, I will get a bottle and hang it from your lower lip. It will get stuck there forever and you'll have to walk around with a bottle on your lip for the rest of your life."

My mother used to tell me that. She also said that I shouldn't swallow cherry pits because a cherry tree would grow out the top of my head. But I liked that idea, so I swallowed every one.

After a silence that lasted five breaths, my grandmother dropped my wrist. She said, "It should have been me that died. I don't mean that in a guilty or sentimental way. She was fifty. Simply from a chronological standpoint, it should've been me."

I didn't know whether she wanted me to agree or disagree. I remained silent, as her fingers once again pressed up and down my arms, feeling the density of me.

"She was never supposed to get fifty years. Most of her life was a bonus. The hole in her heart grew as she grew. Then when she got hit by lightning as a child, it left a scar on her wrist, but also it changed the way she viewed the world. Everything became a story. She told stories to make sense of life."

My mother had told me many stories, but they were always about other people, not herself.

"She was never supposed to get married and have children. The quad-mesters remake a body."

I couldn't stop myself. "They're called trimesters."

My grandmother's hand clamped on my wrist. She led me to sit on the couch, then pushed on my chest and laid me down on the firm seat cushions.

"In the West, maybe. Here there's four: the three of gestation, then the month after you give birth where you regain yourself."

The realization felt like a physical pain. "Mother risked her life to have me and Ainara?"

A wooden drawer creaked open across the room. I heard the clinking of bottles and the rattle of tins. My grandmother's footsteps approached again.

"Why did you never tell us?" I asked.

She parted the hair at the crown of my head and inserted an acupuncture needle. It felt like the sting of a mosquito. My mother had said that only female mosquitoes bite, that they needed blood to have children. People were no different. I thought about my sister's pregnancy. About David's joy at every child we met on our trip, from the boy on the train to Lien.

My grandmother tapped more needles into my head, along the centerline where my hair parted, then added another in my forearm. "Ainara knows. She figured it out when I trained her in the Traditional Chinese Medicine portion of her degree. This tiny hole grows and it shrinks and it grows again. It moves. It's why you never knew your grandfather. It moved from his mother to him and from him to your mother."

"You should have told me."

"You were still a child when you left China. What good would it have done?"

"I was eighteen."

She tapped a needle into my shin. I gasped. This was not a mosquito bite but a wasp sting.

My grandmother drummed a circle around the point with her fingers and the pain stilled to an ache. "Eighteen is a child. Would knowing have made a difference? If you'd known, would you have acted any differently? No, but you would've worried more, felt more guilt. Been less able to open yourself up to your new life."

I wanted to say something bright, but nothing came to mind. It seemed cruel, yet it was true. Since I didn't know how fragile my mother was, I had been able to live freely, to pursue my art and my love. But my sister had known.

My grandmother hummed an ancient Manchu lullaby as she waited for her needles to do their work. "Life happens the way it's meant to happen. You will see this clearly," she said, as she removed each needle. "Not right now, maybe. I can't fix you with this one treatment, but the needles will help you eventually find a balance."

❦

AFTER AINARA GOT back from work, I convinced her to go for a walk in the neighborhood. It was nice to feel the warmth of her hand in mine, leading me slowly through the streets that sounded now more like New York City than the village where we grew up.

I said, "Why a letter? Why didn't you call?"

"I did call. I got silence. I sent the letter the same day. I thought, even if it took time to reach you, at least it was on its way."

"You should've tried again."

"I did. Three more times. I got a busy signal, then a bunch of static, and then it just rang."

Ainara should have gotten my answering machine. Or maybe she'd tried after I threw the phone against the wall.

"I wish you'd kept trying."

There was a long pause, and Ainara's hand tightened in mine. The beeping and honking of cars told me we were at a crossroads. "What difference would it have made? Mother was already dead."

"I had a right to know."

"You think it was mean of me? Did you ever stop to think it was a kindness? She was dead. There was nothing you could do. And until you found out, you could keep living your life happily, in your *new* country, with your *new* people."

My little sister had become so incisive. And she was right: until I found out that she had died, I went days without thinking about my mother. When I did think about her, it was with guilt and regret, so I extinguished the thoughts. "Every time I called home for Chinese New Year or the Moon Festival, I hoped that Mom would pick up the phone. But she never did. It was always you, or Yen, or Dad."

We walked again, her holding my arm steady as we stepped off the curb. "She hated talking on the phone. She said it was like talking to a machine and not a person." Ainara's tone grew gentler. "Every year when your birthday came around, she'd sit on the door stoop and look toward the West."

"I wanted to be sure I'd be welcome before I came back. I thought things would resolve over time, but . . . I don't know. Years slip by while you look the other way."

Ainara grasped my shoulder while a bicycle bell dinged close by. "Did you really never stop to think about it? People get older every day. When you live far away, chances are you won't be there at the end."

"I never did."

Ainara dropped her hand and sighed. "You can be right here and still not be here. I wasn't there for her. We had dinner and Mother said that she was tired. She went to bed an hour early. Dad said she was fine when he went to bed." Ainara sniffed and we stopped walking. "But when he woke up in the morning, she was dead. She'd died in the night, and he had no idea how long—"

"Oh my god."

In shock, I had defaulted to English.

"She didn't suffer. She wasn't sick. She didn't lose her mind in old age. She died in her sleep. That's what everyone wants."

"I thought everyone wants to live forever."

"Grow up, Aimee. We're not children anymore. We know that there's an end to everything, even if we don't talk about it."

"It's been so long since we've talked without counting the minutes," I said. Long-distance phone calls to China cost $3 per minute. Despite my protests that I could afford it, my family never wanted to waste money.

Desperate to make a connection, I tried to reminisce instead about our childhood. "Remember the New Year's when Aunt Eyun brought Jian home, and you threw the frozen persimmon at me?"

"Why would I throw a frozen persimmon at you?"

"You thought I would catch it, but it hit me in the ribs instead." I smiled—a peace offering. "Mother floated the persimmons in cold water to thaw them out and told us to wait half an hour. We didn't want to wait, so I chopped one open too early, and we ate it half-frozen." I waited, but Ainara said nothing. "Remember I told you persimmons have many tongues inside, and that if you eat many persimmons you will be able to speak other languages."

There was a long pause. "I don't remember that. Mother always put frozen persimmons in cold water to thaw them out."

I frowned. How could she not remember? "Mother didn't *always* do that. There was a first time."

Silence. My hands opened and closed on nothing, my palms hot and fingertips cold. "We were young, and you were younger than me, so maybe that's why you don't remember."

Ainara gave a short sniff. "My first memory is from when we went to Ice Dragon Mountain with Mother and Yen to search for ginseng and Feng followed us and got us lost."

I shook my head. "No, Feng found us and led us home."

"That's not how I remember it. That was the day I decided Yen and I were going to be married when we grew up, but then I worried Feng's madness might rub off on him. I didn't know then you can't catch madness."

I felt I was catching madness, learning memories I thought we shared had existed for all these years in my head alone.

We had been sisters in our childhood but were strangers now.

I had to ask. "Was I a good sister? When we were children, I thought I was."

"I looked up to you. You knew many things I didn't."

"I made up some of it."

Ainara snorted. "I figured that out later."

"I wanted to set a good example for you."

"Because you were older, you did everything first. You got good grades first, so I was told to be more like you. You got skinned knees first, so I was told to be less like you. Sometimes, I only knew what I was because I wasn't you. When you left, I didn't know what I was anymore."

"*Dui bu qi.*" Sorry. I didn't know what else to say. Words filled the inside of my mouth, but they may not have been genuine. I had hurt my sister and hadn't even known I had.

She said, "I'm sorry too. But you had to go."

I didn't know how to understand this. Why was she sorry? She was glad I had left?

"You were seeking something that didn't exist here. Eternal Spring was never big enough for you."

My shoulders shook in silent laughter. "It seems too big now."

"But it's still small."

I nodded. "In New York, I wake up in a new city every day. I take photos of the people on the street, trying to capture a moment forever."

"I liked the photo you sent last year, of Shakespeare in Center Park."

"Central Park."

She huffed away the correction. "What do you do with the photos after you take them?"

I took a deep breath. "I try to fall into them. I could when I was a child, but not since." Not since I left for New York. By going to the place the magic was created, I thought I would get closer to it. But instead it got farther away.

"What do you mean?"

"Inside the world of the photo, I walk around other times and other realities. It's a way into a third world. Not America, not China, but a world created of light."

"But you can't anymore?"

"No, and I don't know why."

Ainara squeezed my hand.

I said, "On my eighth birthday, Mother took me to have a portrait taken in the village square. I fell into a photo of New York. That's when I knew I had to go there."

The silence lasted four steps and we stopped walking. Pedestrians and bicycles passed us. "We had a photographer's studio in Eternal Spring?"

"Don't you remember? It was part of a traveling caravan."

She let go of my hand. "No. Mother never took me for a portrait."

I wanted to say, "I don't know why she took me for a portrait and not you, and I'm sorry. I've missed you." But did I miss the sister of my childhood or the sister before me now?

The sister of my childhood looked to me for wisdom because I was older and had a lot to say. She was gone, as surely as the River of Stories washed away words and tumbled them downstream to someone else's shore. The sister I had now . . . I couldn't miss her, because I didn't know her.

"I'm sorry I wasn't here. For Mother or for you."

Her words were angry, but her tone contained no heat. "You left as soon as you could, to pursue your dreams. You weren't here when Mother fell and injured her hip, or when she got pneumonia and vomited blood, or—"

"Ainara—"

"You have a way of seeing things I don't, and you create beautiful art. But artists get off easy. You don't stay and burden yourself in dirt and shit, illness and age. You don't worry about the everyday. I don't fault you, but what I *have* is the everyday. I'm doing the best—"

"You're doing great. I sometimes wish I were more like you."

"No, you don't. Because then you wouldn't be like you."

"We're not so different. We're sisters and we come from the same place."

I heard a key turn in a lock. We were back where we started.

Ainara's cold hand touched my shoulder. "You couldn't have been the daughter who stayed and I could never have been the one who left."

I said the only words that seemed appropriate. "*Dui bu qi.*" Sorry.

TWELVE

My parents came to America for our wedding. My grandmother said she was too old to travel, and my sister stayed home to care for her patients, since she was expecting to see us the following month in Eternal Spring, where she would meet David and host another wedding for us—one all our family and friends could attend.

David insisted on renting a car so that my parents would be more comfortable on the trip into Manhattan. While he circled the terminal, I shifted my weight from my left foot to my right in the arrivals building, ready with my camera, watching the seconds tick away on the overhead clock.

Every time the sliding double doors leading from the baggage claim whooshed open, I squinted and focused my camera. When the frosted doors were closed, I could see the soft edges of ambling bodies, and then they opened and a stranger would appear in Technicolor. My heart leaped with every new person, as first a drip and then a stream of strangers came through.

Not my parents. Not my parents. Definitely not my parents.

I wondered who each of the people around me was waiting for. I made up stories. The white woman dressed as a Buddhist monk was waiting for a disciple. The girl who repeatedly tugged at her knit cap was waiting for a long-lost brother. The man with a bouquet of red roses was waiting for a lover.

My arms grew tired from moving the camera between my heart and my eyes every time I thought my parents might emerge. My forefinger ached from holding its position above the shutter release button.

After a while, I wondered what my life would be if I awaited someone else, the next person to step out from those doors. What if the woman with the deep tan and fuchsia bowler hat was my sister? What if the middle-aged man in jeans and a biker jacket was my husband? What if the older Chinese woman with the hand-stitched hems and the woven blue plastic bag was my mother?

Her bewildered eyes scanned the crowd. I blinked again and dropped the camera. I was so startled I did not take a photograph, the camera dangling from its strap.

My father came to stand beside my mother, both now surveying the crowd.

It had been only four years since they'd sent me off to school in New York, but those years had changed them both. She had swollen around the middle, resembling a Russian nesting doll more than my svelte mother. Her cheeks were hollow despite her new weight, a shadow held under each eye. My father seemed taller but thinner, the dress shirt tucked into his belted waistband ballooning. His hair held an equal amount of white and black.

My mother's eyes skipped from face to face. I thrust my arm into the air and waved. She stepped forward as I bounded toward her.

I hugged her because I had become so used to hugging David's family, my camera digging into us. I grimaced and pulled it to my side. I hugged her again. At first, my mother held her body rigid, but then she returned my fierceness with gentle pressure on my shoulders, patting me then pulling away.

I hugged my father as he tried to shake my hand, which was awkward for both of us.

"Hello, Mother and Father. Welcome to New York."

They took a moment to look at me. No doubt I had changed a great deal in four years too. "Hello, Aimee."

My father nodded. "You look well."

We were shy and awkward with each other—strangers who knew they were family.

As we approached the car, David got out and extended his arm. This seemed to make sense to my father and they shook hands, each smiling but also assessing. Next David extended his arm to my mother. "Mrs. Wu, welcome to New York."

My mother frowned. She spoke and I translated. "Chinese women keep their last names after marriage, so my mother is not Mrs. Wu."

"Oh. I'm sorry." David opened the rear door of the car, and my parents climbed in as I got into the front passenger seat. David loaded their luggage into the trunk, then drove us toward our apartment.

I turned in the front passenger seat to better see my parents. "How was your flight?"

"Long," my mother said.

"Not too uncomfortable?"

"No."

"This was your first time flying, right?"

"Yes," said my mother, as my father said, "I've flown before."

"When?" I asked him.

"A long time ago, in the military."

"Where did you fly to?"

"It doesn't matter," my father said.

I changed the subject. "I'm sorry Ainara couldn't come."

"Hmm," said my mother. Then after a pause, "He's tall, your Da-Vi-De."

I smiled, turning to look at David's head almost touching the roof of the car. "She says you're tall." He chuckled.

"How tall is he?"

"Six foot two. Um, one hundred eighty-eight centimeters."

My mother pursed her lips. "That's too tall. He can't be very smart. The heart has to work too hard to get blood to the brain. Though having two eights in his height number is lucky." She said the number with a northerner's slang, *Yao ba ba* meaning one-eight-eight. It sounded like *Yao fa fa,* meaning getting rich, rich.

My mother now had one hand in the air, gesturing as if lecturing to a class. "But you're only one-five-nine centimeters. That's a big difference. I'll have to consult the book of *Yi Jing* to see if you two are a good match. And, if so, to set a fortuitous date for the wedding."

"Actually, I'm one hundred sixty-five centimeters now. I grew my sophomore year."

She was silent for a long moment. "I'll have to consult the book based on your new height. At least I still know your birthday."

I winced. "You should rest and enjoy yourself while you're here. Also, David's mother has taken care of all the wedding arrangements, so we can't change the date. And I don't believe in the *Yi Jing* anyway."

"Yes, yes, scientific, you and your father."

My father patted her leg. "It's a done thing. Do not fight gravity."

My mother gave my father a sideways look.

"How is Grandmother?"

"She's fine, fine."

"And Ainara and Yen?"

"They're fine."

"And Grandfather Feng?"

"Also fine."

I asked after my aunt Eyun and uncles and other family members. According to my mother, they were all fine. After a few minutes I gave up trying to make conversation, and my mother closed her eyes.

My father looked out the window, craning his neck when we passed a particularly interesting structure. I could see his mind analyzing the buildings, breaking them down into their latticework of pedestals, plinths and pillars.

I imagined him thinking of buildings unbuilt, lives unlived. His hometown of Beijing was a city like New York, and while I'd never thought about that in my childhood, I wondered now if he missed his home. I hadn't questioned why an architect would choose as his home a village where nothing could be built. For a child, wherever you are is the center of the world.

THIRTEEN

I always thought that two separate things had caused my estrangement from my mother. But after I went blind, I saw that they were intimately intertwined.

During Thanksgiving of my senior year in college, David asked me what I wanted for Christmas. I said, "Film."

When I asked what he wanted, he actually sang his answer: "All I want for Christmas is you."

I understood photographically what he meant literally.

I booked a studio in the art department at Columbia University, taped a do-not-disturb sign to the door, and locked myself in.

I set up one of the school's Hasselblad medium format cameras on a tripod and hooked it up to a long wire trigger. I unrolled a background of 11 percent gray paper, a thick stock that rippled with the sound of crashing waves. It ran in a fluid, continuous piece, so the photos would show no seam where the wall met the floor.

I had managed to take twelve credits of photography focused on the streets, the architecture of the city, and the progression of people through the landscape, but had never worked in a studio. Or taken a photo of myself.

I fetched a white plastic mannequin with an unusually slim figure and East Asian eyes. We called her "the Ghost," and she was a mystery because no one knew how a Chinese mannequin had come to live in the studio.

I placed the Ghost in the center of the background and tested the strength and quality of light with a light meter held close to her face.

"Tilt your face higher," I instructed, as I moved her chin half an inch. The light meter went off with a pop. Close, but a ray too bright.

I walked back to the camera and made adjustments. The Hasselblad used square 2-inch x 2-inch film, much larger than the usual 35mm. The larger film size recorded finer details.

The wire trigger was cold in my hand, like an earring found under a sofa cushion. I loaded Polaroid film into the Hasselblad and clicked off a shot.

I fought the urge to shake the Polaroid. Shaking forced the chemicals together so the image developed faster, but it also caused errors and runs. Instead, I held the Polaroid to my heart, warmed the emulsion with my body.

I'd had a vague notion of time prior to becoming a photographer. During the developing time of Polaroids, I counted my heartbeats and learned the length of a minute.

In the darkroom, while I loaded film into the developing canister and prepped chemicals, time dilated to the air entering and exiting my body. In the printed photo, time had the grace to pause.

After thirty seconds, I lifted the Polaroid to my eyes.

The Ghost's overexposed skin shone in a full-body halo. Since I was not a white plastic mannequin, I figured I had the exposure just about right.

I removed my clothes.

It was December 21, the shortest day of the year. Outside the velvet-curtained windows, it was beginning to snow. Through a crack in the drapery where the fabric refused to meet, flakes drifted up in an eddy, caught at a precipice, then glided out of view.

Steam pipes clanked an irregular rhythm, radiating metallic heat.

Despite the warmth, I shivered, and goosebumps rose on my shoulders and thighs. I turned away from the camera, offering it a vista of my back and long hair. I clicked the trigger, the line connecting it to the camera hidden by my leg.

I pulled the Polaroid from the camera, feeling foolish as I held it to my naked heart. My hair emerged first, a dark river between the shores of my shoulder blades, tapering to a point above my tailbone. My legs emerged next, longer than I had imagined them.

This was how the camera saw me. And because I was both before the camera and behind it, this was how I saw myself. I traced the fall of my hair, the balance of my hips, the curve of my instep.

I tucked the Polaroid into a folder in my backpack, then loaded the camera with black-and-white film. I was using Ilford HP5 Plus, a 400 ISO speed film. In my late-night street photography, I pushed the film to 3200 ISO. This allowed me to shoot in near darkness and print grainier photos, showing a grittier reality than reality could hope to supply.

In the studio, I tricked the film in the opposite direction, pulled it to a finer grain 200 ISO. More details revealed. The images would emerge with a sheen wherever one edge met another, where the boundary of self met the world.

I faced the camera and clicked. And clicked. And clicked.

I spent all night in the darkroom, measuring chemicals with weights and hope with heartbeats. By the end of the longest night of the year, I emerged from the darkroom high on alchemized art and chemistry.

I made no changes in the process from negative film to positive print.

The image was perfect because it was me, created by me.

THE PRESENT I gave David during the Hilton family Christmas ceremony was a leather-bound volume of Greek myths, with a bookmark at Prometheus. It was how we met, arguing in literature class about the meaning of light. He gave me a case of photographic film the size of an ottoman, with a Post-it Note that read, "For taking a photo you can fall into."

Later that night, by moonlight in the guest room, I gave him my real gift. "You said all you wanted for Christmas was me."

He didn't say anything for a long moment. Then he laid down the photo and kissed my fingers. "Why is there a ribbon on your pinky finger?"

"It's a red ribbon. My mother used to say Laoyue, the old man of the moon, ties an invisible red ribbon of fate to everyone. On one end is you, on the other is your *dui xiang*. Soul mate. It's much more poetic in Chinese."

David knelt on one knee. Like a magician doing a coin trick, he waved one hand in front of the other. On the tip of his forefinger appeared a single diamond set in a gold band. "Amy Wu, will you marry me?"

I remembered that my mother said marriage was not just about the man and the woman, but about the man's family and the woman's family.

I shook my head to clear it of all thoughts that were not happy thoughts of David and me and our future together.

"Yes."

FOURTEEN

My mother dealt with jet lag by alternately giving in to the urge to nap and defiantly staying awake late into the night. Then she gave up. "I'm going back to China soon anyway, so why try to adjust to New York time? I'd have to go through this all over again when I get home."

She frowned at English-language television, asked questions about the homeless on the streets, and said the water tasted different in America. She also thoroughly inspected the back of David's head when she thought no one was looking.

My father took to New York as if the city was his spiritual home. He said it reminded him of Beijing, a city full of architectural wonders. He carried a sketchbook everywhere and strolled through the streets, drawing buildings and people.

My mother woke me during the second night to say that my father was not in bed. I stayed up with her and told her stories about my misadventures in college. He returned with his sketchbook three hours later.

She confronted him. "I was worried about you. You don't speak English and I was afraid you got lost."

He tucked his sketchbook into a drawer. "The streets are all numbered. How could I ever get lost?"

The next night, he went out sketching again.

TWO DAYS BEFORE the wedding, my mother came to the doorway of my room. "Aimee, I want to talk to you."

I folded the chapel veil I'd been holding and laid it across the pillows. My mother sat on the bed and patted the space beside her. I sat.

"What is this?" Her fingers slipped through the layers of silk.

"It's my veil. It's bad luck for the groom to see the bride's dress before the wedding day." I reached for the veil and inexpertly laid it over my head. The edge trailed across the bedspread and onto the floor.

She frowned. "It's white."

"Of course it's white."

"Bad luck, white. You look like a ghost or like you're in mourning."

I smiled, threw my head back, and felt the veil slide down my shoulders. "In the West, wedding dresses are white."

She folded her hands in her lap. "Aimee, you can't marry Da-Vi-De." She said it as if it was a new idea that had just popped into her head. We both knew it wasn't.

I narrowed my eyes. "What do you mean, *can't*?"

"I'll tell you a story and you'll understand. Your aunt Eyun always loved with her heart unfurled, like the petals of a flower." My mother gestured, her fingers blooming open.

I knew this. "She's very passionate. She used to visit me when I was in high school in Harbin to tell me about her love affairs."

After many years of falling in love with the wrong men, she finally fell in love with the right one and got engaged. They booked a banquet hall in Harbin because there were no buildings large enough in Eternal Spring to hold their guests.

Did my mother worry that I was cutting off my Manchu roots as Eyun had?

"Eyun's getting divorced," Mother said.

She had married only a year ago. "What? She didn't say anything in her letters."

"Listen, she met this wonderful man and fell in love. She met his family, and they hated her, but no matter, they got married anyway. He was sure his parents would grow to love her. Naturally, they all lived together. Everything Eyun did was wrong, and everything was her fault." My mother leaned closer and lowered her voice. "Everything her husband did wrong was her fault too. Things his parents had tried to change about him for years were, all of a sudden, her fault. Since she was his wife, they reasoned, she could get him to do whatever she wanted. When she tried to talk to him about their concerns, he called her a traitor, and accused her of plotting with his parents against him."

"She divorced him."

My mother laughed, tears collecting at the corners of her eyes. "*He* divorced *her*."

I scowled. "I hope he gets what he deserves."

"He's remarried already."

"Then I hope she gets what she deserves. She can remarry too."

My mother looked thoughtful for a long time, then said. "No, Aimee."

"Why?"

"Do you know what the difference is between men and women? Women only get one chance. If you miss it or mess it up, that's the end."

"What? You're being cynical."

"How many divorced men do you know of in China?"

I thought for a moment and counted out loud. "One, two, three . . . four."

"And how many divorced women?"

"None. Well, now Eyun." I tilted my head and considered this.

"Where are the women those men divorced?"

It hurt me deeply that my mother was telling me a story about divorce two days before my wedding. I shook my head. "I don't know."

My mother raised a finger in the air, as if accusing heaven. "Nobody knows, because the women don't stay around long enough to tell anyone about it. All the divorced women ask for job transfers to other towns, then lie about their past."

"The stories you told when I was a child were better."

"So you see why you can't marry David?"

I pretended that I could no longer follow the thread of my mother's thoughts. "David's family loves me. They would never blame me for—"

"You know that's not the point of the story. Eyun's mistake is that she left Eternal Spring. She could have stayed and married a childhood friend. Now look at her: all career and no love. Far away from her family."

"That's not her mistake." Eyun's mistake was not going far enough away. My mother and my sister are lucky; they were born where they belong. My father, Eyun and me, we had to find our homes.

"If you marry Da-Vi-De, you will never return home because this will be your new home. This wedding . . . I won't allow it."

"This isn't about you, Mother. It's about me and my choices. I'm going to marry David." I stood, a hand to my heart. It beat hard against my palm—in defiance, in fear, in love I could not make her understand.

"He's not your *dui xiang.*"

"David is loving, intelligent, kind—"

She sighed. "Not for you. He's not right."

"He loves me. He makes me happy."

"Happiness isn't everything."

I knelt and took her hands in mine. The joints of my mother's index fingers bulged, and cuts marked the base of her thumbs. The four lines of her lightning scar glowed in the light of the setting sun slanting through the window blinds.

"Happiness *is* everything. How happy have you been in this lifetime, Mother?"

She snorted but didn't pull away.

"How many times have you smiled until your cheeks hurt? How many times did Father tickle you until you couldn't stop laughing and had to gasp for breath?"

I couldn't remember my parents ever openly expressing affection. They were cordial and amicable with one another, but not demonstrative.

"It's easy to seem happy when all you do is go out to fancy restaurants and shows," she said. "It's easy to be happy when everything is good. What happens when things are bad?"

"Why are you assuming that things will be bad?"

"Don't be childish, Wu Aimee." She only said my surname first when she wanted to emphasize that I was Chinese. That I belonged to her.

"People call me Amy here."

"He can't even pronounce your name. He says it Amy, lightly. One word. Not strong, not two words. Ai-mee." She pressed her hand against her chest with each syllable.

"It's different here, Mother. I can't go around correcting everyone all day long, making them say my name over and over again."

"But he's not just anyone, he's the man who loves you, right? Wu Aimee, he doesn't even know you."

"*You* don't know me! You don't realize that I'm not a child anymore. You can't make my decisions for me. I'm not Manchu, I'm not Chinese, I'm not American. I am all of them, because I am me. And if, as you say, he can't understand me, then neither can you. Neither can anyone." I squeezed her hands. "He loves me. Isn't that what counts?"

She looked away. "You don't know love."

"Listen to me, Mother. David loves me. He tells me every day."

"Americans love everybody and everything," she scoffed. "I love your scarf. I love orange juice in the morning. I love—"

"He not only tells me, he shows me. I believe him. I love him too."

"It's easy to say love, love, love all day long. You wear out the word."

Anger flared in me. I tried to tamp it down, but the feeling exploded until it thrummed in every finger and every toe. "If it's so easy, then why don't you ever say you love me?"

"I'm your mother. You *know* how I feel. All mothers love their daughters."

"I've never heard you say it."

"Of course I love you, Aimee."

I closed my eyes. Sometimes when you wait too long for something, the reality of it doesn't measure up to the expectation.

"Then let me make my own decisions. I'm marrying David."

She recoiled as if I'd slapped her. "I don't understand you."

"You don't have to understand me, Mother. You only have to love me."

"I'm your mother. How could I not understand you." It was not a question.

My parents didn't attend our wedding. She changed their plane tickets, and they flew home the day I married David.

I was so angry with her that the following month, we didn't return to Eternal Spring.

FIFTEEN

After breakfast one day, I tried to talk to my father. I turned to him as if I could still see. I didn't know how long it would be before I accepted my blindness. I wasn't good at acceptance.

"Father, please talk to me."

Wooden chair legs scraped the tile floor. His footsteps retreated. Had I not heard that, I would have known he was gone by his scent fading, that unmistakable mix of charcoal and turpentine. In my childhood he was always drawing and creating.

I gripped the edge of the dining table and forced myself to my feet. I trailed my fingertips along the wall to navigate the hallway, following the scent of creativity—black pepper pencil lead, toasted linseed oil, the umami of uncured clay.

When I reached the source, I hoped to pass through an open doorway. Instead, I met a solid piece of wood. I felt around for the doorknob and entered.

I imagined my father now the king of a nation

populated by art supplies such as we had never known when I was a child.

I heard him sigh across the room.

I stepped forward, arms out, and walked toward his exhalation.

"No!"

Too late.

My bare foot hit something crisp and hard, which smashed against the floor. Disoriented, I swayed, and stepped forward.

Pain and wetness. The scent of copper joined that of oil and turpentine.

I wanted to say I bloomed with blood; that it spread from the cut, and the red color was stark against my pale skin. But I couldn't say any of those things. Bloom, spread, red: all things seen with the eyes. My artistic language. "I'm so sorry. I seem to have broken something of yours." *Dui bu qi*. I had said it to Ainara and I was saying it again.

I felt around at chest level. Would I find something to hold on to or something else to break?

My father's hand caught mine. He led me three steps. "Sit."

I sat. He left the room.

I was so ashamed. To have chased him blind and then broken something of his! I hoped the floor was of a dark-colored wood, so I wouldn't ruin it with my blood. I lifted my foot to feel the damage. A jagged piece of something sticking out of it pricked my finger.

I heard my father come back.

I chewed my lower lip. "I'm so useless."

He swatted my hand away. "You're not useless." Warm, wet softness greeted my foot, as he cleaned the cut with a towel. He prodded my toes with his fingers. "It wasn't deep. You won't need stitches."

"Thank you." I could feel him tense, and I did too. Chinese people don't thank their family. What they do for you, they do without thanks. You only thank strangers. I fumbled for words. "I mean . . . what did I break?"

"It's not important."

I reached for him, but my hand met air. "Of course, it's important. Tell me what I broke."

His tone was flat. "A sheet of glass."

He moved away and I heard the clink of glass on glass. Each piece of different size and shape resonated with a unique sound as he piled them together. The pieces bonded by blood made the deepest sounds.

"Why was there a sheet of glass in the middle of the floor?"

"I was painting it." He left the room again.

A sick suspicion clenched low in my belly. A broom swished to the tinkling of glass shards. The metal dustpan amplified their chiming.

"You should've listened to your sister and worn slippers in the house." He had changed the subject, but I was happy he was talking to me about anything at all.

"Wearing slippers indoors makes me feel like my feet are bound."

"Better bound than bleeding."

He left the room again.

I explored the table next to me, which held many sculptures made of clay that fit perfectly in the palm of my hand. Most were dry, but one was malleable under my fingertips. It was about the shape and size of an egg, but with grooves cut into the sides.

A shock of familiarity. When my father had helped me and Ainara make monthly calendar pages as children I'd seen some of the unrealized architectural designs in his precious sketchbook. The grooves I felt on the clay surface were the metal latticework of the building. An egg-shaped high-rise.

I fingered other sculptures. One had many sharp points jutting from a solid cube center. Another resembled a pagoda, but with more exaggerated curves and swoops.

I didn't hear my father return. When he patted my back, my shoulders hitched in surprise. "These are your buildings," I said.

This time a warm, damp towel brushed my foot, followed by a bandage. He picked up my hand and turned it to where I had pricked my finger, but he didn't stick anything on it. "They're just models."

When he tried to pull away, I hung on to him.

"I know. But you made them." I caressed the egg model with my other hand. "They were drawings before and now they exist in three dimensions."

He pulled his hand away.

I tried not to be hurt by his withdrawal. In my childhood, my father was endlessly supportive of my ambitions. He'd been proud of me when I left.

I didn't know how to interpret him now.

I CALLED MY aunt Eyun, the only other phone number I knew in China by heart. She had returned to Eternal Spring five years earlier, when the oil boom hit an inflection point. Her expertise with lasers was now used to direct drilling equipment.

She said she would be over immediately. A minute or an hour passed.

I still had sound and scent and textures and flavors, but my relationship to those senses was frail. I had made a career of seeing more than other people. Not seeing ate me from the inside out and found my flavor lacking.

David answered the door. I stood from the couch and was nearly knocked over by a female body hugging me until my lungs compressed. "Aimee! It's been so long. You grew fat!" In Chinese, saying "you grew fat" was a way of saying that someone seemed healthy and not lacking for food.

I hugged her back. Eyun let me go after several heartbeats. "How do I look? Have I aged much, or am I still the same?"

I'd told her on the phone of my blindness, and now I blinked several times to reinforce the idea for both of us. Eyes open or closed, the world was dark. "I'm sure you look exactly the same."

She laughed. "Yes, well, better you stay blind then. I'll always be as you remember." In English, she said, "Hello, my name is Eyun. I am Aimee's niece." She paused. "No, Aimee is my niece. Her mother is my sister."

"You speak English," David said.

"I read English better."

He laughed. "I can't speak or read Chinese, so you're way ahead of me."

I was profoundly relieved that Eyun could speak to David without needing me to translate. We had written to each other in English when I was in high school, because she wanted to help me learn. I hadn't known her spoken English was still so good.

"How did you learn?" David asked.

"I'm a physicist. I need to read the work of English and Russian scientists."

"You're trilingual?"

"Quad: Manchu, Mandarin, English, Russian."

"*Way* more useful than me. I only speak English and some Latin I learned in college."

"Who do you speak to in Latin?"

David chuckled. "No one. It's a dead language."

Manchu was dying like Latin. My mother and her childhood friends were the last to speak Manchu as a native tongue. Younger Manchus spoke Mandarin Chinese as their mother tongue and only picked up a few words of Manchu along the way.

"Amy has been urging me to learn Chinese."

"*Ai. Mee.* Her name is Aimee."

"Aimee." David spoke my name as if tasting an idea. "I've always called her Amy."

I tilted my face toward their voices. I remembered calling home a few days ago and saying to my father that I was Amy. Him hanging up on me because that is not my name.

"Amy's a regular name in America. Aimee sounds similar, but Amy is easier."

Eyun scoffed. "Easier, maybe. But not correct. What does Amy mean?"

I smiled. "It's French for 'beloved.'"

"David, what does your name mean?"

"It's Hebrew for 'beloved.'"

Eyun laughed, a deep-throated rasp full of humor and sensuality. "You call each other the same thing but in different language? Beloved and beloved?"

David and I laughed too. "David, you should learn Chinese. In Chinese 'beautiful potential' is *Ai mee* and 'beloved' is *Ai ren*."

His clothes rustled, and a pen clicked. He said to Eyun, "Here, please write the two in Chinese on this Post-it Note."

"Hello, brother-in-law," Eyun shouted in Chinese so it carried across the room to my father.

"Hello," my father said as his footsteps retreated.

"What's wrong with him?" she said. "He enters the room. He leaves the room."

"I'm going to speak English so David will understand but Father won't. It's not you, Auntie. He's angry with me. I think I broke his light for the Moon Festival competition by accident. I want him to win."

"Zero problems. I will go peek at the blueprint and we can rebuild."

I opened my mouth, but David stilled me with a hand on my shoulder. "She's tiptoeing to your dad's room."

"Where is he?"

"Standing in the doorway to the kitchen, watching her tiptoe to his room." David chuckled.

I smiled.

Eyun soon returned and whispered. "It's broken, not destroyed. I know how to fix."

"What are you up to, Eyun?" my father asked.

Eyun called, "I needed to borrow a pencil and you always have supplies."

Eyun, David and I left the house for the market. On the street, all the tiny hairs on my arms stood in response to the change in temperature and humidity. It was raining what my mother called *mao mao yu*, raindrops so thready and gentle that when they touched my arm, it felt like a ladybug walking across my wrist.

"We should bring an umbrella," David said.

I shrugged. "Not for this kind of rain. My mother would've said it's enough to touch your skin but not enough to touch an umbrella."

"She would say the Nishan shaman ridiculed her assistant for using an umbrella in such rain, a waste of the air trapped underneath," Eyun added.

I kept my eyes closed now because keeping them open was worse. When they were open, I blinked too much, as if each blink held the possibility for seeing. When my eyes were closed, I could believe that it was my eyelids that hid vision, not my grief.

My grandmother's acupuncture relaxed me but did nothing to help me see. My sister hadn't given me more than that one cursory check. I guess all our childhood joys had been a dream.

David tucked my hand in the crook of his arm. "I'll make sure you don't bump into anything unless it's me. You can bump into me as often as you want."

I had held his arm this way many times, from walking down the aisle to walking through Central Park while fireflies lit up a summer evening.

"What a pair we are! Me blind and you mute in Chinese," I said.

"David is only mute in Chinese and Manchu. He speaks Latin." Eyun cackled.

The sound of motorcycles and birds and street vendors singing the names of food assailed us.

David said, "I think we're a great pair. Between us we still have all our senses."

I took a step forward—not long enough—then took another that was too long. After a few steps, I'd grown used to his body next to mine. Every dozen steps, I opened my eyes for a moment, hoping to see the road beneath our feet, to see whether I had veered left or right.

"You're doing great. It's like you've been walking for years," David teased.

"Maybe I'm cheating and I can actually see. Maybe I'm saying I'm blind so you'll have to take care of me."

"Tomorrow you can pretend you can't taste anything, and I'll cure you by feeding you all my favorite foods."

"You mean all *my* favorite foods, not *your* favorite foods."

He chuckled. "That's what I said, all *my* favorite foods. Hey, is that Grandfather Feng?"

I tilted my head as if by doing so I could see. "I don't know."

Eyun sighed deeply. "Yes, it's Feng."

I could tell David was waving from the way his body shifted. "Feng de Feng!"

"That's rude," I said.

"Isn't that his name?"

Eyun said, "No. Feng de Feng sounds like 'the Mad Feng.' And his name is not the word Feng meaning madness, but Feng meaning pinnacle."

"Oops," David said.

I had never seen Grandfather Feng's name written down, so I didn't know which Feng he was. I smelled dried leaves and barbecue lamb, then heard a chipper voice. "Aimee! I see you've found your mother."

I had known Feng my whole life, yet his words still caught me by surprise. "This is my aunt Eyun, not my mother."

"*Ni hao*," David said.

"Nee-Haooo." Feng copied David's pronunciation, dragging out the sounds. He shook my free hand, as if in the prelude to a business meeting. His skin was dry and thin; it slid and crinkled over his knuckles. "Is your mother enjoying the Land of the Dead?"

"I don't know. What did she say the last time you talked to her?"

Feng laughed hard in my face, his breath hot. "The last time I saw her, she told me to put on a jacket and not die from catching a cold. I don't know if she's enjoying the Land of the Dead, because I listened to her."

"What did he say?" David asked.

I shook my head and translated.

"What did he say?" Feng asked.

I told him what I was thinking instead. "You led us in a circle all over town and then to the wrong house."

Feng harrumphed. "I led you to exactly where you needed to be."

"That's not where my family lives."

He drew out the word. "No. But it's where you live."

"I live in America."

Feng guffawed. Drops of his laughter tapped my forehead. "Translate. It's funny."

I frowned as I translated.

"David doesn't understand why you think my mother's alive when she's dead."

"That's because he's a Westerner. He lacks the Manchu way of understanding. Right now, you also lack the Manchu way of understanding." I felt the pressure of a dry fingertip on my forehead, in the place where Buddhists say the third eye resides. Feng tapped three times. "Look! See!"

A cricket chirped.

"I'm blind!"

"Exactly."

"I—"

"He's gone," Eyun said. "He skipped away and is now hiding behind a scooter across the street."

"That seems in character."

David cleared his throat. "It's a child's scooter, so Feng isn't really hidden."

I smiled. "That is extremely in character. Can you point me in the right direction?"

I held my disposable camera at chest level.

David squared my shoulders, and I took a photo of Feng.

THE SCENTS OF garlic and earth, roast pork and cantaloupe, diesel and dish detergent enveloped us. Shouts in Chinese and Manchu, vendors hawking the names of produce, meat and cookware.

Eyun said, "The old outdoor market was here before: vegetable sellers, fruit sellers, the egg seller who ate raw eggs, the man with the oven on his back."

I smiled as a memory coalesced. "I remember. But he didn't stay here, he traveled door to door. Mother would give him a bag of corn or millet and a coin. He'd whistle, then throw the grain into a heat-tunnel machine he carried. After a few moments, he'd pour out popped corn or millet as a treat."

David laughed. "A door-to-door millet popcorn maker?"

I nodded. "It was pretty great."

"It was pretty great," said a nasal voice I didn't recognize.

"Are you making fun of me, David?"

A bird cawed. "Making fun of me, David?"

"I swear it's not me." The parrot copied David before he had finished speaking, their voices overlapping. The word "me" echoed for long moments.

A man said in Manchu, "Take the parrot, please!"

Eyun said, "We're not looking to buy a parrot."

"But you must!" A hand grabbed my sleeve. As Eyun tried to draw me away, the man said, "This parrot has been in my family for generations. It is immortal, but it doesn't do us any good because it doesn't speak Manchu or Chinese. Only English. Please take it!"

I shook my head while Eyun translated for David and the parrot echoed her words.

I pried the man's hand off my sleeve. "I don't want a parrot. Even an English-speaking one."

"Although it is quite a party trick," David added.

The parrot said, "It *is* quite a party trick."

I frowned. "Let's go. I don't see how talking to a parrot gets us anywhere."

The parrot echoed me. "I don't see." Then with a loud caw at me: "See!"

WE BOUGHT PANES of glass, translucent paint, brushes and glue. Considerate of my blindness, Eyun placed each item in my hands so I could feel it before David packed it into his backpack.

As we left the market, I heard the parrot simply cawing, since there was no one speaking English nearby.

I said, "I hope fixing Father's light will help him forgive me. I wasn't here—"

"He needs to forgive himself. He *was* here," Eyun said.

"What do you mean?" David and I asked at the same time.

Eyun stroked my hand as we walked, but she spoke to David. "Aimee's father was born in Beijing. While studying architecture in university, the Down to the Countryside policy of the Cultural Revolution started. Students and intellectuals were sent to rural areas for re-education in the ways of the farmers. He met Aimee's mother, but was careful not to get attached. Years went by. Their feelings grew. When they married, he lost the Beijing residency paper, got the Eternal Spring paper. Then the policy changed and he couldn't get his Beijing paper again. He was stuck."

I stopped walking. I knew my father was from Beijing and had come to Eternal Spring in his youth. I hadn't stopped to think about why an architect would come to a village on the edge of nowhere, with no electricity and nothing to build. "He hates it here."

This time, Eyun's words were directed at me. "He doesn't hate it. He liked it when it and your mother were the only choice." She paused, choosing her words carefully. "Had he waited another month before getting married, he would have had other choices, because that's when the policy changed. He could have chosen to return to Beijing by himself. Your mother always wondered if he regretted staying with her in Eternal Spring."

THAT EVENING, I sat at the dining table before dinner while Lien did homework. Her pencil scratched against paper, the sound broken by the swish of an eraser, then the puff of air as she blew the eraser's scraps away.

"Auntie, what's America like?"

"What do you mean? Don't you see America on TV?"

Lien patted me with her small hot hand. "Of course I do. But it's not real. TV shows about life in China aren't how we live, so why should TV shows about America tell you what America's really like?"

"You are wise." I thought about it for a long moment, brow furrowed. "Tell me what you think China is really like?"

"China is a wonderful big country full of my family, and I'm proud to live here. My family takes good care of me. I love my school and my friends."

America is like that except it's a country where none of my family live except for David. "America is a big country full of diverse people who believe in something called the American Dream. For most people, it's about being financially successful, but everyone calls themselves middle class even though some are rich and some are poor."

"My American Dream would be for everyone I know to be healthy," Lien mused. "And I want to eat candy without getting cavities."

"Wouldn't it be a Chinese Dream because you're Chinese?"

"But you're my auntie and you're American, so I must be a little bit American too."

I nodded. "Good point. But if you're going to be a little bit American, you should understand what the US Constitution promises: life, liberty and the pursuit of happiness. That means that everyone should be free to choose what they want from life, and what most people want is to be happy."

"That's strange. If you live a good life and you never hurt anyone, obviously you'll always be happy."

I smiled, missing a time when my own life was so black and white. "I don't think it's possible to never hurt anyone. But you're welcome to try."

"You talk pretty straight for an adult. If I'd asked Grandma to tell me about America, she would have told me a story instead." Her grandma, my mother. Lien sounded sad.

"Do you want to hear a story?" I asked.

She squeezed my hand in answer.

"Okay, once upon a time—"

"What year is once upon a time?"

I frowned and she giggled. "Western stories don't begin with the dynasty and year," I said. "Once upon a time means a long time ago, but we're not sure when. So, once upon a time, there was a man named Odysseus who had won a war in a faraway land and wanted to return home. When he began the journey, he had twelve ships, but they were driven off course by storms. They landed on an island full of lotus, and a cyclops captured them."

"What's a cyclops?"

"A monster who has only one eye."

"That's not nice, to pick on someone with a disability."

"The cyclops is born with one eye. He is large and mean and eats people."

"Ah well, you can pick on him then."

"Odysseus and his men blinded the cyclops with a wooden stake and escaped. But Poseidon, the god of the sea, was the cyclops's father. Poseidon was angry and cursed Odysseus to wander for ten years."

I heard the sizzling of oil, then smelled garlic and ginger being fried in the kitchen.

"If he could've sailed home directly, how long would it have taken?"

"A few weeks, with a good wind."

"Ten years is a very long time, then. It's more years than I am."

I nodded. "Yes, it is. The master of the winds gave Odysseus a bag that would help his journey. His crew thought there was gold inside the bag and opened it, creating a storm that drove the ships farther away from home."

"Oh no!"

"It gets worse. They came across some cannibals who destroyed eleven of the ships by smashing them with rocks. With only one ship and its crew left, Odysseus sailed to the western edge of the world. There, he made sacrifices to the dead to ensure a safe journey home and met several ghosts."

"Are American ghosts the same as Chinese ghosts?"

"No, they're not. And these were Greek ghosts, not American."

"I thought you were telling me an American story."

"I am. It is an American story because it's a Western story. Let me finish.

"The first ghost was of a sailor who wanted to see his body buried. The second ghost was of a prophet who advised Odysseus on how to get home. The third . . ." I stopped as I remembered the identity of the third ghost. I shouldn't have chosen this story. "The third ghost was of Odysseus's mother, who had died of a broken heart waiting for his return."

"She must have loved him very much."

Odysseus's mother had dreamed him into existence long before giving birth to him. Her love was a snapshot of time developed into an image she could hold—the longer he was away from her the more she feared they would never be together again. "He tried to hug her three times, but each time his arms passed through her. She said, 'This is the nature of ghosts: You can't hold us.'"

I thought of my mother, and my hands quivered with the need to hug her one more time. I hid them under the table. "Odysseus sailed around the island of the Sirens, whose song usually pulled sailors toward drowning. He and his men passed safely between a six-headed monster and a giant whirlpool. But then they suffered a shipwreck, and everyone except Odysseus drowned. He survived by clinging to an uprooted fig tree floating in the ocean and washed up on the island of a woman named Calypso."

"What's a fig tree?"

"It's a tree that grows figs. You know, Adam and Eve and the fig leaf. The fruit."

"Never heard of it, but okay, if you say so."

It seemed so strange to me Lien had never heard of a fig, but it was a tropical fruit that would never make it to the market in Eternal Spring.

Now the smell of soy sauce and aged black vinegar floated from the kitchen.

"Odysseus stayed seven years on Calypso's island, but he always remembered his goal. He finally met some Phoenicians, who were expert sailors, and they delivered him back home."

"Did his family recognize him? He must have changed."

"They recognized him because he had a scar on his hand from childhood." I thought of my mother's lightning mark. I would recognize my mother anywhere, the Land of the Living or the Land of the Dead.

"Not a bad story. Tell me another."

I remembered a winter when I was ill with the flu and I'd said those exact words. I was feverish and unable to sleep. My mother stayed awake to keep me company. The candle flickered and cast her face into ghostly shapes, stretched her shadow first in one direction then in another. I asked her to tell story after story. And, whispering so as not to wake the rest of our family on the *kang* bed, she obliged. Finally, she'd said, "That's all you're getting out of me tonight. I'm tired and they're your stories now."

I said to my niece, "That's all you're getting out of me tonight."

She giggled. "You sound like Grandma!"

My sister approached with dinner. The smell of fish stew dragged me back to a Chinese New Year when Eyun was in love, when I fell asleep in front of the wok and lit my heart on fire. At last, my mother's voice came to me, a whisper on the wind of memory.

SIXTEEN

My mother told me stories when I was in her womb. She wove threads of words until they turned into a tapestry of consciousness. Until I heard her.

"Hehe Manni created the universe by drumming," she told me. "She took a piece of the sky and made it into a tambourine. She took a towering mountain and made it into her drumstick. When the sky tambourine and the mountain drumstick collided, the great bang of it created men and women and all the creatures."

Another time, she said, "The good heaven mother Abka Hehe battled with the evil Yeluli, then made all people."

And another: "Light of the sun, Ulundun Mother, gave birth to all living things. She created the heaven, the earth, the mountains, the streams and us."

My mother's warm voice caressed me. "Every Manchu person has three souls, so it's all right if each of them believes in a different story of creation."

Now my mother's face appeared in the midst of my blindness. "Aimee, you must see."

❀

I SAID TO Ainara, "I heard Mother's voice."

"I hear her voice all the time. What did she say to you?"

"She said, 'Aimee, you must see.'"

"Too obvious."

I frowned. "What does she say to you?"

"She reminds me to pay the bills, tells me to take Lien to the dentist, gives me recipes for stir-fry."

My mother had only given me one sentence. Still, I was grateful for anything—a word, a grunt, a sigh. I took a deep breath. "Did Mother ever tell you she loved you?"

Ainara's voice came from all around me as she bustled around the room, clanging pots and slapping dishes on shelves. "Aimee, how can you be so smart and yet so stupid? Why would she ever say she loved me?"

"Because she was our mother."

"Exactly. Do you need someone to tell you the sky is blue and the sun is bright?"

I chuckled humorlessly. "Well, yes, now I'm blind."

I caught a whiff of Ainara's peony-scented shampoo. "You haven't always been blind. Your blindness now doesn't wipe out all your years of refusing to see."

I nodded. I didn't want to miss the chance to say to my sister things I wished I had said to my mother. "I love you."

She waited as if I might say more, then said, "I know."

"Do you blame me for not coming home for your wedding?" I asked.

"I didn't go to yours."

It was not the same. Ainara would have had to apply for a passport, then prove financial assets to get a visitor's visa to America.

I felt her stop inches away from me, her breath warm on my cheeks. "When you said you were going to high school in Harbin, I knew you'd never come back again. Mother said you would, but I don't think she believed it either."

"I intended to come back."

"How could Eternal Spring compare to Harbin and art and architecture and museums? We all knew you'd go to university next. I thought you'd go to Beijing. But even our capital wasn't enough; you had to go to the capital of a different nation."

"New York's not the capital of America."

"Doesn't matter. What matters is from the time I was fourteen, I knew you were never coming back." She took a deep breath and sighed it out in a rush. "Why didn't you come home to get married?"

"You know why—I fought with Mother. She didn't approve of David, of my career. She didn't approve of me."

"Big deal."

I nodded.

Ainara groaned, too loud. "I was being sarcastic. Mother also thought I shouldn't become a Western doctor in addition to training in Traditional Chinese Medicine. She thought I would go to school like you and never return."

I frowned. "But you're the good daughter."

"I'm not the good daughter. I'm just the daughter who stayed—because I wanted to, not because Mother wanted me to. Approval isn't the same as love. I have ideas for Lien's life, but she'll grow up and be her own woman."

I reached for her blindly. Her hands caught mine in mid-air. "I've missed you," I said. "Both what we had as sisters, when we were kids, and what we could've had as sisters, now that we're adults."

"In all these years, you've never had a holiday?"

I thought again about the difference in our lives. "We go to visit David's family for Thanksgiving and Christmas. Only for the weekend. In America, there's no week off for Chinese New Year or National Day. I have a week of vacation per year, and sometimes I need to use them for sick days. David and his friend founded a company, so he often works day and night. We never had enough time."

Ainara didn't sound cruel, but her words pierced. "There is never enough time—there is only time."

She hooked her pinky finger into mine, as she had so often done when we were children. "Hook fingers and promise you'll keep coming back."

I curled my pinky and pulled, sealing the deal. "I'll visit, and call and write. Just not in Manchu."

"Is your Manchu so bad?"

"I had to get the letter translated," I confessed. "Why did you write me in Manchu? I was never good at it."

Ainara pulled her pinky away.

Silence. Silence for so long I wondered if she had left the room. "Because our mother was Manchu."

And with the name of our people on her lips, I felt our sisterhood dissolve again.

❧

TOO SOON AND too late, the day of the Moon Festival arrived. It rained the night before—drops of water marching across the metal roof and into my brain. Relentless.

My father, Eyun, David and I stayed up through the night to fix my father's light. He rebuilt gears; Eyun cut and beveled sheets of glass; David stripped wires and soldered electrical components; I sculpted more landmarks from damp yielding clay by touch and instinct. The air in the living room filled with the brazen sharpness of cut glass, the metallic fire of electricity, and the delicious warmth of earth.

I hoped the rain would stop in time for the lantern competition—water and electricity shouldn't mix. For an instant, I thought of my mother's wrist, where the lightning had marked her as a child.

The rain continued through morning. My grandmother and David played many games of chess, using Eyun as a translator. I had worried for years that my family wouldn't accept him, but he was as easy with them as he was with me.

My father and Lien illustrated a calendar for the coming month. I took photos of them, aiming my camera toward the sound of their voices.

A draft blew into the living room, and the rain grew louder. Ainara entered the house. "The rain's overwhelmed the storm drains. There's a layer of water on the street."

I smiled, imagining it. "The street is mercury. Liquid and silver."

A hinge creaked, and I smelled rubber and leather. Ainara said, "We'll have to wear rain boots to get to the festival. I only have one pair. Aimee, you can wear them, and I'll wear plastic sandals."

I raised my arm to stop her. "I'll take the sandals. I want to feel the water."

WE WALKED TO the festival as the rain turned to mist. My grandmother, my father, Aunt Eyun, Ainara and Yen and Lien, David and me. For a day in September, the air was warm. I breathed in diluted water, inhaling the memory of my mother on her favorite holiday.

Eyun said, in English, "This interesting. The River of Stories has overflowed. The street leading to the bridge is underwater. The People's Square hosting the lantern competition is on the other side."

I stretched out a foot in my sandals. The water swirled around my toes, crested over my foot and splashed my ankles.

Eyun gripped my arm. "It gets deeper. Some people are thigh deep in water and turning back."

My mother was dead, but to heal my relationship with my father I had to get to the other side of that river. I had to help him win the lantern competition. "I'll swim across if I have to."

"Hold a moment."

Water sloshed as she walked away. David took my hand. I spoke to him as freely as if we were alone. "When my family scattered my mother's ashes, they flew on the wind and fell in the river, on the mountain and into the earth. She's a part of the rain and the water around us now."

"I read that as time passes, even a buried body becomes atoms that work their way into the environment," he said. "There's about a hundred microns of Elvis in each of us."

I shivered.

David ran his hand up and down my arm. "Are you cold? Looks like there's a bigger storm brewing."

I smiled at the absurdity of our situation. "I'm not cold. But how can you tell there's another storm coming? It's been raining night and day."

He chuckled. "Trick knee, remember?" David had an old football injury that got aggravated when he had a long flight—his knees were always jammed against the back of the seat in front of him.

"I love you," I said as I stretched up on tiptoes. I aimed for his lips but kissed the edge of his chin.

Eyun's voice said, "I need your help."

I turned toward her, but she stilled me with a hand. "Not you. I need David to help me keep the lantern dry." She switched to Chinese. "Lien will be your eyes."

An umbrella puffed open above my head, and David wrapped my hand around the grip. "Just in case."

The beeping of Lien's Tamagotchi preceded her, like personalized theme music on a TV show. "I'm going to tell you everything that's happening like I'm telling you a story," she said. "I'm pointing my finger at the moon rising through the clouds. Grandma used to say the moon is a dot and the dot is a story."

"She told me every dot on a ladybug is a story. Or a laugh. Or a meal. Or a caress."

Beep beep, went the Tamagotchi. "I only care about stories. Because stories have all the laughs and meals in them."

"Yes," I said. "A story is a life."

Rain struck our umbrella, tiny grenades exploding.

Ainara and Yen and my grandmother joined us in the deeper water.

Beep beep. "If a story is a life and I'm telling you a story, does that mean I'm giving you a life?"

I smiled and squeezed her hand. "Yes."

A PIERCING WHISTLE.

Lien gripped my hand and pulled us in the direction of the sound. "Aunt Eyun and Uncle David are back with Grandpa Feng on a boat."

The sound of a motor echoed into the cave under our umbrella. Even with Lien's help, it was difficult for me to decipher the scene through voices and echoes, scents and sensations. But it felt magical.

"The River of Stories is a lake today so I'm going to ferry you across," Feng called. "But be patient. I go slow because I have no depth perception."

I frowned as we boarded the boat. Yen got in first, then took my arm while Ainara steadied me. The ground beneath me changed from solidity to a gentle rocking. "Why does he have no depth perception?"

Ainara said, "He's blind in one eye because of a cataract."

Feng said, "I know all of you. But I don't know you two foreigners. You're not from around here."

I shook my head. "You know me. I'm Aimee."

Feng grunted. "All right. But the white man's not from here. *That*, I'm sure of. Or he's from here, and you are not."

"*Ni hao, wo shi* David." He had learned enough Chinese to say hello, I'm David—a whole sentence. "Tell him thanks for taking us across the river."

I translated, and Feng laughed as the boat moved. "No need to thank. I'm only doing it because no one else can steal a boat. Especially not you foreigners."

"I'm from Eternal Spring! You know me!" I yelled, while Eyun translated for David.

As the rain drummed our many umbrellas, I heard a zipper open or close. A pen click. A scratching against paper. David placed a pen in my right hand and a pad of Post-its in my left. As best I could, I wrote my name in Chinese and English. Then I wrote it in Manchu as well.

I freed the slip of paper and held it up. A cool breeze kissed my fingertips, and the Post-it was accepted.

My grandmother said, "Too much rain. Everything is so slippery."

Beep beep. "Don't worry, Auntie Aimee, you can hold on to me. Four legs are better than two."

Yen said, "The saying is 'two heads are better than one.'"

"But four legs *are* better than two. If I say it enough, it will become a saying."

Laughter all around.

Warm rain dripped off my umbrella and splashed on my shoulder, like the fall of happy tears.

"What do you see?" I asked no one in particular.

Ainara said, "It's a bucket being dumped unevenly over our heads."

Yen said, "It's gray and muddy."

Eyun said, "It's a door curtain made of crystal beads."

My grandmother said, "It's not healthy to get your hair wet in the rain."

"I wish I could see what all of you see."

Yen said, "Remember the story about the three blind men and the elephant? One man felt the trunk and thought an elephant was long and muscular like a snake. Another man felt the leg and thought an elephant was solid like the pillar of a building. The last felt the tail and thought an elephant was thin like a rope."

Beep beep. "They were all wrong!"

Yen said, "Or they were all right. Because an elephant *is* like a snake and a pillar and a rope. It's all those things and more."

"Mother once asked us a riddle about weighing an elephant," I said over the sound of the engine.

Yen laughed. "I remember. An emperor gave his son an elephant as a birthday present. The prince wanted to know how much the elephant weighed, but it was too large for any scale. How did they weigh the elephant?"

It was a difficult riddle, and I hadn't got the solution.

Ainara had, and she said it now. "You put the elephant onto a boat, then mark the amount the boat sinks into the water on the side of the hull. Then you take out the elephant and fill the boat with rocks until the boat sinks into the water the same amount. Then you weigh the rocks and you know how much the elephant weighs."

My family together in this boat probably weighed as much as an elephant.

Thunder cracked distantly, adding a line of bass to the tenor of the rain and the baritone of the engine. Rain fell harder.

I said, "Remember when we were children, we used to count the seconds to calculate how close the storm was?"

Ainara said, "Yes. The closer the storm got, the shorter the time between the lightning and thunder."

I said, "How close now?"

Ainara and Yen counted together. "One, two, three, four, five."

A boom of thunder.

"One, two, three."

I stuck my hand beyond the edge of the umbrella, palm up. The rain wove through my fingers like a caress.

Crack! I smelled fresh ozone in the air. My hair lifted heavenward and tried to float me into another world. My fingertips burned from the kiss of lightning. The thunder was directly above our heads. Lien screamed, then laughed. Beep beep.

Together, Ainara and Yen said, "One."

SEVENTEEN

One autumn day, my mother led Yen, Ainara and me into the forest on Ice Dragon Mountain to hunt for ginseng. A highly prized plant, its root is said to cure everything from old age to heartbreak. Most hunters sold their ginseng at the market, but my grandmother gave ours away to her elderly patients, though she first dried and ground up the roots so her patients wouldn't know they were receiving it and feel indebted to her for such expensive medicine.

Before dawn, we gathered at our front door. Ainara was confused about the plant's name: *Ren* is person. "Is it called *Ren Shen* because the life of a ginseng is like the life of a man, because it gives life to man, or because it gave birth to mankind?"

My mother smiled and patted her head. "It's called *Ren Shen* because it's person shaped. It has arms and legs and a face." She held up a ginseng root in her left hand and turned it slowly. "Every daisy is the same, but every ginseng is different. This ginseng enjoyed dancing. See—it has long limbs and a smiling face. Some have stubby toes and scrunched-up faces. Others are rigid and stout."

When no one volunteered to pose for my father's drawings, he drew ginseng root instead. On paper, the limbs of the *Ren Shen* morphed into a person; stalks and leaves into hair, smudges and dents into smiles and sidelong gazes.

On the street, only Grandfather Feng was awake and toiling, leaning his frail body hard into our street's iron hand pump, trying to gather water in an upside-down bucket. "It's never full," he complained. Water drummed the bottom of the bucket, bounced and fell to the thirsty earth.

Yen righted the bucket for his grandfather, then ran to catch up with us, as Grandfather Feng continued to chant, "It's never full. It's never full . . ."

I asked my mother why it was called hunting for ginseng and not searching for ginseng.

My mother cinched her belt. "Ginseng is elusive, more a tricky person than a plant. It hides well in the forest and can sometimes run away from you."

Halfway down the street, I tugged on Yen's sleeve. "Your grandfather's following us."

Yen turned, and his grandfather crouched behind a chicken as if it would hide him. The chicken flapped its wings but failed to fly away. Yen shrugged. We walked on.

Yen's father met us with his horse-drawn cart at the first intersection. My mother joined him on the front driver's seat. Yen jumped onto the back of the cart, then held out his hand for Ainara and then me. After we were both settled, Yen held out his hand again. Feng climbed in with us.

"Good morning, Grandpa Feng," Ainara greeted him.

Feng regarded her for a moment without expression, then sang a song about a cricket who'd lost a slipper.

FENG WAS THE first one off the cart when we arrived at the base of Ice Dragon Mountain. He ran and hid behind a birch whose trunk was no thicker than my arm.

Yen's father said he'd come back for us just before sunset and returned home.

We walked up the road and into the forest, the earth red under our feet.

I thought of the Chinese word for forest, which was composed of three identical radicals of the word *mu*. One *mu* standing alone is the word tree, two *mu* standing side by side is a cluster of trees, and three *mu* arranged two on the bottom and one on top is forest.

Sometimes Ainara lagged behind to look at a flower or Yen stopped to look for Feng, but always my mother was in the lead. She told us, "You kids are closer to the other world, the world of *tian*, so you can better hunt the ginseng."

Ainara tugged on her sleeve. "But mother, *tian* is the sky. How can we be closer to the sky when we're shorter than adults? And even if we're closer to the sky, how does that make it easier for us to find a root in the earth?"

"*Tian* is both sky and heaven. Ginseng is of heaven, even though it grows in the earth. You kids are newly born from heaven. You can feel the ginseng better than adults who've been on earth longer. We're covered in dust."

"You're not covered in dust—you wash every day."

My mother gave a faint smile. "When a person goes through life, things happen to them. Every day of sunrise and sunset, every time we make a new friend or lose an old one, eat something alive to stay alive ourselves, we move farther from the world of heaven and more fully into the world of earth. It's best to hunt with pure hearts not covered by dust."

The sparse growth underfoot morphed into an orgy of green. A canopy of overlapping branches arched above us. The wind caressed the trees, which in turn whispered to each other and to us. The forest floor writhed, each plant fighting to reach the light. I ran my finger along a curled fern leaf. Most ferns sprouted in spring but this one sprouted in autumn. "Look," I said, and pointed to it.

"Oh, pretty!" Ainara clapped her hands.

My mother gestured all around. "Keep your eyes open for streams. Ginseng grows around streams, especially ones that come from the north or the east."

I smiled. "They're just like us. We're from the north and east of China."

"Also, watch for *Yan Ling Cao* and *Tian Nan Xing*." Age Extending Grass and Southern Sky Star plant. "You can't hunt ginseng by looking for it directly. It's too smart to be found that way, so look for its companions."

"I see one." Yen crouched by a single-stemmed plant topped by a cluster of red berries.

My mother squatted next to him and examined it. "This is false ginseng. The leaves look the same and so do the berries, but it's not a real ginseng. It will have no scars."

"Why do we want ginseng with scars?" I asked. "Isn't it better to find one that's perfect?"

"No real ginseng is without scars. Every year, the ginseng grows a new stalk from its root. This stalk leafs out and receives energy from the sun during spring and summer. Then, in late autumn, the leaves give up all their sweetness to be stored in the root, so the plant can survive winter. When the stalk falls, it leaves a scar. You can tell how old a ginseng is by the number of its scars."

I saw a glittering of tumbling crystals through the trees, and we walked toward the light. It was a seasonal brook that cut diagonally from the northeast. We followed it upstream.

Ainara pointed. "Look! I see an Age Extending Grass and a Southern Sky Star plant."

The stem of the Age Extending Grass was topped with a trio of perfectly spaced leaves. Growing less than an arm's length away was a Southern Sky Star plant, its leaves making the shape of cupped hands drawn by a master calligrapher.

Within kissing distance of the Southern Sky Star was a ginseng.

Ainara and I jumped for joy, and Yen nodded his head and smiled. My mother knelt next to the plant. Sifting the soil with her fingers, she exposed the root. "It has scars! One, two, three . . . it's fifteen years old, so a good age to be harvested."

My mother removed a hand trowel from her belt and drew a wide, shallow circle around the ginseng plant. "This moat is so the ginseng doesn't run away. It locks it in and tells us where to dig so we don't break any roots."

"Ginseng can run?" I asked.

My mother replied in all seriousness. "Faster than you realize. They go back to heaven and are gone forever."

"Is it bad to break roots?" Ainara asked.

"Yes. Every ginseng must have all its roots, big and small, to be effective. It's aware of all its roots like you're aware of your fingers and toes."

I wiggled my toes.

My mother wiggled her fingers. "Each one of its roots is important, because each reaches for something different."

I spread my hand and saw that my fingers pointed in different directions. If I followed the path from my fingertips they would never cross.

"If you break even one tiny root, it will lose its sense of self. The ginseng won't know where it ends and the dust begins. A confused plant is bad medicine. It can't make a person well again."

Yen and Ainara and I freed our digging forks from our belts and loosened the soil around the plant, being sure not to break any roots. A quarter-hour later, my mother plucked up the fat ginseng, its bulbous body swaddled in dozens of hair-thin roots that cascaded from the crown.

She immersed the ginseng in the stream, letting the cold water wash away the dirt. After it was clean, she showed us the scars: fifteen distinct diagonal marks.

My mother put the root in her satchel and walked on.

I waved my arms in the air. "Wait! If we found one, there must be more ginseng here."

My mother shook her head and smiled. "No, Aimee, you won't find another ginseng here. When one is gone, the land where it lived weeps and cannot support another for many years."

"But wild grapes grow with other wild grapes."

My mother shook her head. "Ginseng does not grow with other ginseng."

Yen tilted his head as we followed her. Dappled sunlight fell on his face. "How lonely."

Ainara nodded. "To never be near others like yourself your whole life. I wouldn't know what I'd do if you all weren't with me."

I thought about this. "Maybe the ginseng does have people like it around all the time. The Age Extending Grass and Southern Sky Star enjoy the same environment. Just because they don't look the same on the outside, doesn't mean they aren't the same on the inside."

My mother glanced back at me as if I was becoming a person she no longer understood.

"Father told me a person's life is dependent on five things." I counted them on my fingers. "Fate, luck, character, environment and education. Your fate is your fate; you can't change it. You can predict your luck based on previous experience. You can improve your character. You can change your environment. You can advance your education."

Ainara shrugged. "I'm glad I don't have to worry about relying on any of those things. I have you and Yen every day."

WE FOUND SIX more ginseng. As the sun slid to the western horizon, we retraced our steps down the mountain. The temperature dropped slowly but steadily and my mother's grip on her ginseng bag tightened. We couldn't find the road.

Ainara shivered and hugged herself. "I'm cold."

My mother took Ainara by the hand and we walked on. Every now and then I cupped my hands over Ainara's ears and warmed them by rubbing her earlobes.

When my mother spoke, her breath formed a cloud. "Let's stop here for a rest."

The four of us sat on a fallen tree. I hugged my knees for warmth.

Feng jumped out in front of us, his arms aloft. I gasped. I'd forgotten he had come to the forest.

He said, "What are you looking for?"

My mother waved in greeting. "We are looking for the road."

"And have you found it?"

My mother shook her head. "I used to come hunting for ginseng with my father when I was a girl. I should know the forest well. But the mining changed it."

"How long have you been looking for the way home?"

"A long time."

Feng tapped his temple. "Then I see your problem and your solution."

"Do you know the way?"

Feng laughed, his saliva spritzing the air. "No, but I know you haven't found it by looking for it. The solution is obvious: don't look for it and you'll find it."

I crossed my arms. "Grandfather Feng, that doesn't make sense. How can you find something by not looking for it?"

Feng walked in the direction from which we had just come. "Follow me!"

My mother got up and hurried after him. "We can't let him keep wandering the forest by himself. It'll be dark soon. If Feng doesn't follow us, then we must follow him."

"We're all going to get lost!" I moaned. "You can't find something by not looking for it."

"Lost, lost, lost! Don't look for home and you will find it. Lost, lost!" Feng shouted.

"We're already lost!" Ainara ran and held our mother's hand.

I muttered so that only Yen could hear. "We're going to freeze to death when night comes. It's not possible to find something by not looking for it."

Yen took my hand. "Trust him."

An hour later, following Feng, we found the way home.

EIGHTEEN

David said, "We're walking under a covered walkway to the People's Square." Rain drummed the metal roof, a thousand ghostly fingers playing a half-remembered melody.

Beep beep. "Auntie, we are walking to the ultimate contest." Lien sounded very serious.

Voices rose all around us, singing.

Some sang in Manchu and some in Chinese, but the meaning was the same. It was the song sung every year to open the Moon Festival. The soprano peaks merged with baritone valleys, the highs and lows filling each other until all that remained was harmonious togetherness.

I remembered the tune but not the words. Fingers still tingling from my brush with lightning, I joined the song in Manchu, grasping for the lyrics. David hummed along as best he could. Voices tapered away until only the children remained, their high last note dissolving into gasping breaths and giggles.

"That was beautiful," David said. "What does the song mean?"

"It's about Eternal Spring, the mountain and river and heaven and earth. I haven't sung it in half a lifetime and don't remember many of the lyrics."

Lien said, "Now the competition can begin."

There came the sounds of motors turning, light switches flipping on, whispers and murmurs from the crowd and questions from the judges.

"Auntie, I'm going to go look at the other entries."

"Lien, you can't go off by yourself. It's not safe."

"I'm not by myself. I'm with my whole family."

David whispered, "Your grandmother's shadowing her. She'll be okay."

I nodded. A breeze blew damp hair across my cheek and into my mouth. I sucked on the rain-soaked strand, tasting the peculiar sweetness of autumn rain.

"Describe my father's light to me," I said to David.

"It's an octagon three feet tall by two feet wide. Each face is a layer of frosted glass. In the center is a light connected to a power source. Inside the lantern three rings rotate independently, and on them sit architectural models and paper cutouts of human figures."

I wanted to see my father's creation. "Mother used to tell me the story of the Nishan shaman," I said. "When she first crossed the River of the Dead, she gave the ferryman, who was blind in one eye, a slip of paper with a word on it as payment. When she returned, she had no more slips of paper, so she restored sight to his one blind eye."

"That's a powerful shaman. Maybe we could get her to restore your sight. I have lots of slips of paper to pay her."

"It's not about money."

"I'm talking about Post-its."

I laughed.

I was skating on the edge of a thought that tickled, but in my blindness, I couldn't reach it without hearing it out loud. "During a solar eclipse in my childhood, my father told me that to see I had to not see. Don't see the sun by looking directly at it. I had to look instead at the reflection it casts."

I thought of my mother, giving the tube of athlete's foot cream to Yen's mother. I thought of her seeing so poorly that she memorized the eye chart, and yet she was the most perceptive woman I knew.

Water vapor surrounded me, like a mother hugging her child at the end of a long day. I breathed it in and it became a part of me. My mother's voice said, "Aimee, you must see."

My mother was right.

I closed my hands and concentrated on the lantern that would soon be lit before me. Had I gone blind because I had not wanted to see the sadness and judgment on my family's faces?

I heard my mother's voice in the thunder. At first it whispered, then spoke, then shouted.

I lifted the disposable camera to my face, as if I could see, thumbed the advance gear—despite knowing I wound it after every photo. The texture of the saw-toothed wheel grazed my thumb as I directed the camera toward the sound of my father's voice.

"You cannot see light," my father said to Lien. "You can see what it does, but not what it is."

I closed my eyes for a moment, then opened them. I took a photo.

I told David, "When I was a child, I'd go outside on moonless nights to say hello to the stars. I'd close my eyes to better adjust from the candlelight inside the house to the dim light of the stars."

"The light of the stars isn't dim. It's your distance from them that makes them appear that way."

When my camera's shutter closed, I was in a world of darkness. And yet I saw. I understood—I knew what my sister was doing and my grandmother too. I knew what my father's lantern looked like, not because I'd seen it with my eyes but because I knew him in my heart.

I heard my father flip the switch.

Gears turned. The three rings inside the lantern rotated, each at its own speed. The outer ring held the buildings of Eternal Spring as they are now and might be in the future; the middle ring the buildings of Eternal Spring as they were in my childhood; the inner ring cutouts of people from history and legend who had inhabited Eternal Spring throughout the ages. I knew this and so I could *see* it.

As the rings revolved, the Nishan shaman and Sergudai crossed the River of Stories and emerged in People's Square. Laoyue, the old man of the moon, sauntered past Ice Dragon Mountain and appeared next to my father's egg-shaped skyscraper. My mother stood next to our old house for a moment, then sashayed into the People's Square of Eternal Spring, to where we stood.

"What a beautiful feat of engineering," David said. "I wish you could see this."

I squeezed his hand hard. "It's beautiful."

David turned to me, frowning. "You can see?"

I shook my head, but clasped my heart, smiling so hard I was on the verge of laughter. "I just know."

I stood the same way as my mother, right foot turned out, one hip higher than the other.

The lantern revolved and cast shapes and light into the world. The light spoke to me in my mother's voice. "We are all who we are in this moment, but also who we have been in the past. You belong."

The Nishan shaman and my mother walked through us and among us. The light of the lantern was the sun, and all of us were the moon, reflecting rays as a photo would, as a story would.

I could see with my heart.

I backed out of the group of people, moving instinctively, so that David would be included in the frame. I took a photo of my family.

Time had the grace to pause.

A judge whose voice I had not heard before noisily flipped back and forth through the pages on his clipboard. "What do you call it?"

I looked at where I knew Ainara and Yen stood. In my mind, they were children.

The shadow of my mother flickered between my father and grandmother, as large as life. I looked over at David, and he was himself at six years old, helping a pigeon to fly again.

When my father spoke, I knew, from his voice, that he looked as proud as he had during that Moon Festival competition in my childhood. He said, "It is the light of Eternal Spring."

My father won the Moon Festival competition.

NINETEEN

Despite breaking my father's light, I had helped him fix it again and win. I smiled until it felt as if my face would never know another shape.

When I awoke the next day, my eyesight had been restored. I acknowledged this, but not with the relief that I had expected—I knew now that I could see without sight. After I wiped the sleep from my eyes, I studied my hand that had touched lightning. Four red lines were etched in branching paths on my wrist. The lightning had developed a photo on my skin.

I marveled that it didn't hurt, but instead felt warm like a hand holding mine.

MY FATHER ASKED me to help him take apart his lantern. I knelt beside him on the floor of the living room. "It's too beautiful to destroy," I said.

He said, "It's served its purpose. Art is a moment in time—with enough years, even the Great Wall crumbles."

I nodded and slipped a pane of glass out of its frame, then I reached in and pulled out his sculpture of the River of Stories.

"Remember your mother's story about the Nishan shaman?" he asked.

I thought of the many versions she had told me. "I do, although she told it to me in many different ways. I once asked her which one was the truth and she said they were all true."

My father removed the sculpture of Ice Dragon Mountain. "One time she gave my name to the Lord of the Dead to check if I was listening."

I laughed. "She rewrote the story in her head every time. I miss her."

He lifted out the translucent paper sculpture of my mother. "I miss her too."

I caressed the recreation of the People's Square, a miniature echo of the place where the competition had taken place. "I remember helping you with your lanterns when I was a child. Well, I never was much help. All I did was catch some fireflies and keep your secrets."

My father stopped spooling a red wire and looked me in the eye. "That was what I needed."

We worked on in silence until the lantern was broken down into glass, electric components and sculptures.

My father tucked the paper cutouts of the Nishan shaman, Laoyue and my mother into his sketchbook. On the left-side page, he had drawn a face in profile, a woman with ginseng hair and a faraway, unfocused gaze.

It was me.

My father closed the book. He fetched a box and we packed away the parts of his lantern. He took a deep breath before picking up the box and carrying it to his room.

I loitered in the doorway, shy to enter. "I'm sorry I wasn't here." He waved vaguely. "I want you to understand why I left." I fetched my purse and pulled out the photos I always carried with me. I laid them out on my father's drafting table. "I think you may understand better than anyone."

The first photo was of me as a child in front of a painted backdrop that made it look like I was riding a bicycle in a lake. "On my eighth birthday, Mother took me to the photographer's studio, to have a record of me on that day."

My father stood beside me and traced the shape of the lake with his finger. "I remember this day. You were so excited."

I pointed to the next photo. "When I was at the studio, I fell into this photo of New York City." I had touched it and fallen into it so much in my childhood that the corners of the paper were round. I explained to him how falling into photos made me feel, what it meant for me to have found not only New York City but a world all my own.

My father's head snapped up. "Why didn't you tell me?"

"I didn't know how to say it. I told Grandfather Feng and he said I wasn't crazy but a shaman. But that sounded crazy, so I kept it a secret."

My father pointed at the next photo. "Who is this child hugging a pigeon?"

"That's David."

"And you've fallen into this photo also?"

"I haven't been able to fall into photos for many years. I take photos every day trying to create one I can fall into."

He nodded as if this made sense to him. He pointed to the last photo. It was a side profile of a woman I had stalked with my camera in the streets of New York City last year. "Who is this?"

"She looked like Mother. I thought . . ."

My father said nothing for a long moment, but the wrinkles at the corners of his eyes flexed. He touched the photo of me on my eighth birthday.

"I should have tried to talk to Mother more about what my art means to me, why I love David, why America is my home."

My father picked up the photo of the stranger who resembled my mother. He sighed. "This doesn't look much like her. Your mother didn't smile this way in photos."

Lightning struck again.

"What photos?"

"All of them." He opened a cabinet and drew out a thick photo album. "Yen bought a camera years ago."

I had never imagined—

The truth was I had never imagined. In the years I'd been away living my life, my mother had also been living hers.

We were so poor in my childhood, I had never seen a photo of my mother. And so I assumed there were no photos of her in the world.

With quaking fingers, I opened the album and saw my mother on every page.

I gasped. I touched each with reverence, my fingers barely grazing the prints. The sharp ninety-degree edges scored my hand as I stroked them.

There was my mother on her birthday, blowing out candles on a cake piled high with glazed fruit. My mother when Lien was born, her hair frizzy around her face. There was my mother in Harbin on holiday with Ainara and Lien and Aunt Eyun, her cheeks wind-chapped during the Ice Festival. Dressed in new clothes for the Chinese New Year. Here was a whole life my mother had lived without me.

Looking at these photos, each a story of her life I didn't know, I cried. My mother had many good years after I left for America. She had many good years after we were estranged. She had not died of a broken heart.

Among the photos of special events was a snapshot that captivated me.

My father leaned in to look at it. "That was our thirtieth wedding anniversary. Ainara bought a cake, and Lien stole one of the strawberries before we could cut it."

In the photo, my mother sat with my father on the couch in the new living room. They held hands. Lien's laughing face took up half the foreground, giant and out of focus. The camera captured my mother with one hand up to wave.

"She looks so happy."

"It was a good day."

I held it at arm's length. My fingertips frissoned with the heat of contact. It traveled electric up my arm, into my shoulder, then into my chest—igniting all my cells.

I smiled.

Rain falls. Snow falls.

I fall.

I emerge in the living room. My mother and father sit on the couch together. Ainara is directing and Yen holds the camera. Lien styles my mother's hair, brushing it with a doll's brush, then pushing it over her shoulder, bringing it forward and curling it, then braiding it. My mother takes the attention without protest.

She looks at my father, then around the room, at the straight walls and the solid ceiling, at Yen and Ainara discussing the photo layout, at my grandmother holding a newspaper, at Lien still fussing with her hair.

Even though I know I can only inhabit the world of the photo for a short time, I walk toward my mother. She turns to my father and whispers. "Can you believe it's been thirty years?"

He nods. "More than thirty if you count the time before we were married."

She bats the air with her hand. "I don't, because you hadn't yet made up your mind to stay." My mother's gaze falls to her lap. "Although it wasn't a decision, because you had no choice."

My father takes her hand. "There's always a choice."

Lien shakes the hairbrush in frustration. "I can't get it right. I need it to be perfect."

My mother reaches out to still Lien's hand and says, "You don't have to make it perfect."

"But if I don't do it perfectly, you'll be upset, and you won't forgive me."

My mother tugs Lien into her lap. "In the Song dynasty—"

"We learned about the Song dynasty in school this week. It was from 960 to 1279."

"Yes. In the Song dynasty, there lived a duke named Han Qi. When he was on a military campaign, he asked a night watchman to bring a candle so he could write a letter home. The night watchman was not careful with the candle. He set Han Qi's shirt on fire."

"Oh no!" Lien swats my mother's heart as if to put out a flame.

"The next day, Han Qi noticed he had a different night watchman. He went to speak to the supervisor."

"Did he ask if the new man was better than the old one?"

"No, he asked to have his old night watchman back. Han Qi said, 'Having made a mistake, he has learned and so will not repeat it.'"

Lien purses her lips and twirls a strand of her own hair around her finger. "But he might make other mistakes. Isn't it better to start all over again with a new person?"

I am standing behind Lien when my mother speaks, and it feels like her words are for me. "The night watchman will make other mistakes, but he will learn and grow as a person. If Han Qi hadn't forgiven him, he wouldn't have that chance."

My mother stands to slide Lien off her lap, and her eyes meet mine. "So, you see, you have to forgive people when they make mistakes. And you have to forgive yourself."

I say, "I'm sorry I wasn't here. I miss you. I love you."

She sits again and says, "I'm ready for my photo now."

Ainara and Yen smile and a flash illuminates the room. Time stands still. The bright light digs into every shadow—in front, behind, between my parents.

I fall out of the photo.

I was still standing with my father. He looked at me with a smile. "Did you see her?"

I nodded.

My father said, "She was my favorite person in the world."

I REMEMBERED WHEN my mother taught me to write the shape of the universe.

Whenever I bothered her while she was busy, she gave me assignments. In the beginning, I would write a single sentence, unrelated and fanciful.

She urged me to write paragraphs, saying, "Many people can write a good sentence, but not many can tell a good story." But I was more interested in doodling in the margins, drawing the little circle that is the Chinese period that ends a sentence.

My father had left a metal ball bearing on the dining table. I drew a small ball at first, then a larger one when the ball rolled toward me on the uneven surface of the table. Over time, my circles grew larger. I lost interest in writing words and didn't bother Mother when she was busy, simply continued to draw circles.

I tried to improve my hand-eye coordination by drawing the ball without looking at the paper, keeping my eyes firmly on the object itself. My first attempts were mangled ellipses, the end of the line not even touching the beginning.

When I complained to my grandmother, she laughed. "Aimee, only mad people can draw perfect circles. Don't worry. You will improve."

This struck me as odd. Did she mean I would improve but never be able to draw a perfect circle because I was not mad, or I would one day be able to draw a perfect circle and then *be* mad?

Feeling like a spy from the fall of the Qing dynasty, I tiptoed next door to Yen's house with a piece of paper and a pencil. Grandfather Feng sat at the dining table, picking his teeth with a needle. I placed the paper and pencil on the table between us. "Please draw a perfect circle."

He squinted at me, studied the sheet, then removed the needle from his mouth and stabbed the paper. He held it close to his eye and peered at me through the tiny hole.

A perfect circle.

My mother said, "Words and stories are the building blocks of everything. By learning to write a sentence and then a story, you can write the shape of the universe."

My father scoffed when I told him this at breakfast the next day. "You'd better understand the double helix then, or decipher a fractal. Learn to draw a Möbius strip. That is the shape of the universe."

He cut a sheet of paper from his sketchbook and folded up the bottom inch. He tore off the thin slip of paper, turned one end over and glued the ends together with rice porridge from his breakfast bowl. The slip of paper now resembled a calligraphic number eight.

My mother frowned but didn't say anything.

My father gave me a pencil. "Draw a line down the length of the paper and see what happens."

I drew a straight line. My pencil kept going long after I thought I should have reached the end of the paper, until the end of my line touched the beginning of my line. I was surprised to find both sides of the paper bore my mark.

He nodded. "That is the shape of the universe."

In bed that night, I lay illuminated by a shaft of moonlight that held me in place between my mother and father. I turned and tucked slips of paper and drew invisible lines with my finger.

Lines that went on forever, crossing over and over the point of origin.

TWENTY

The camera sees both ways; it sees the world before it and the person behind it. What I photograph is as important as what I remember.

The beginning of summer was the moment of cicadas, their instruments an orchestra that floated on the wind.

The middle of summer was the moment of mosquitoes, stealthy predators metallic from stolen blood. My mother told me all that I needed to know about mosquitoes. "Wear light-colored clothing," she said, "loose enough so the air buffers and protects. Use *qing liang you* mint oil on your forehead to guard against bites. Stay indoors during sunrises and sunsets. Mosquitoes bite children because of their sweet blood."

Ainara said, "That would be why they like me better! Because I'm younger and sweeter."

I frowned at her as my mother laughed. I don't know why I was competitive about being bitten by mosquitoes.

I had never told David what I was waiting for when I said I wanted to have children in the future. Now I knew that I'd been waiting to feel whole, to be all Chinese and all American and all me, to fall into photos again. To create a photo I could fall into.

By the end of summer, the world belonged to ladybugs. As the sun set, the brick western wall of our house gleamed a welcoming orange. A few ladybugs would land on our wall, then a few more, until the wall became a living tapestry. As the evening deepened into night, they departed one at a time. By morning they were gone, only to return in the afternoon.

It was the season of the ladybugs now.

Late in the afternoon of our last day in Eternal Spring, Ainara said, "Come for a walk. There's something I want to show you."

David and Lien came with us, holding hands. She pointed at objects and taught him their Chinese names, while he taught her their English ones.

We left the house and walked east. The banks of the River of Stories had receded. We walked across the bridge to the end of Convenience Drive and stopped at the store that used to be our childhood home.

Ainara led us around to the western wall of the building. "When they built the store they tore everything down, but these bricks were okay, so they left them. Do you remember?"

The section of wall was six feet wide by four feet tall, and the bricks were darker than the rest, with deeper grooves etched by rain in a pattern of memories. When Lien touched the brick, Ainara said, "Your aunt Aimee and I once lived here."

Lien giggled. "You lived in the store? That must've been very convenient. You'd never run out of candy!"

"It wasn't a store back then, it was a house. When our grandparents built it, they could only get enough red bricks to make a part of one wall. The rest of the house was made from straw bricks."

A ladybug landed on Lien's shoulder and climbed her like a mountaineer. "Is that a brick the color of straw?"

"No, it's brick made from straw."

Lien giggled, a child wise to the jokes of her mother. "That's not a real thing. That's a story about pigs. The straw house, the wood house and the brick house."

"A straw brick *is* a real thing. You cut the straw, then beat it into mud and set it in a mold to dry in the sun. Once it's dry, you have a straw brick."

The ladybug flew from button to button on Lien's dress. "You can't make bricks out of mud. It would fall apart as soon as it rained."

"Then how do you make bricks?"

Lien thought for a moment, then sang out, "With a machine from the TV ads. Buy a brick-making machine, make bricks, sell bricks, make money. Call 800-138-87283212—"

Ainara laughed. "All those machines are is an oven. Mud is what gets baked in them."

They waited while my translating caught up.

"They have TV ads here for brick-making machines?" David asked, and I translated.

Ainara turned to him and nodded. "Oh yes. Chinese people are very entrepreneurial these days."

"But how many people would want to buy a brick-making machine?"

Ainara laughed. "Some will buy noodle-making machines

and others will buy window-making machines, and others will buy bookbinding machines."

Lien said, "And some will buy pigs, and some will buy sheep, and some will buy chickens."

We all laughed.

"Ainara, the day we arrived, we ran into Feng on this street," I said. "He led us in a big circle from here and back because he said this is where I live."

"You know Feng doesn't always make sense."

I smiled and looked at the river from which my mother had fished so many tales. Late afternoon sunlight skipped on the surface like gold coins. "But he was right. I was living in the past."

Our eyes met and Ainara nodded.

I said to David, "Please buy Lien some candy. I want to talk to my sister for a minute."

After they disappeared into the store, I said, "Grandmother told me the tiny hole in the heart grows and travels. It went from our great-grandfather to our mother—"

"You don't have it."

I looked at the ground. "I know. Does that mean you do?"

She nodded. "I don't know when my heart will stop."

I placed my hand on my sister's heart, then picked up hers and laid it on my own. "None of us knows how long our heart will keep beating."

Ainara removed her hand. "It's beating now. That's the only way to get from one day to the next."

The sun began to set. The golden hour photographers are supposed to prefer, but which I'd always found annoying, descended on us. After days of blindness, I was overwhelmed by the orange light on red brick. The mortar lines flashed the color of orange marmalade.

I touched my sister's stomach, where her future child dreamed. "I'll come back when your baby's born."

David and Lien exited the store, each holding a skewer of sugar-coated hawthorn berries. As Lien bit into hers, the hard sugar exterior cracked with a sound like ice breaking across a frozen lake. Half the berry ended up in her mouth and the other half flew from the skewer to land on the street. Lien scowled.

Ainara led us to a crescent-shaped stone bench near the bank of the River of Stories, and we sat. The river boiled with colored carp, red and gold and orange interweaving an endless pattern.

I leaned forward, catching a fragment of reflection in the constantly moving surface: a strand of hair, a shoulder, my disposable camera held up to take a photo.

Through the camera, I saw the river, the fish, the reflected sky and all of us.

Each photo was a frozen moment, a pattern of living fish and rippling water that will never repeat.

"What are you looking at?" Lien asked.

"The fish. Do you know about permutations?"

She looked at me, puzzled.

I got up and knelt by the river. Reaching into the water, I pulled out two dripping stones and laid them side by side. "If you have two stones, there are only two possible permutations." I switched the stones.

Lien nodded. "One stone first or the other."

I groped in the water for a third, pink and shaped like an egg. "If there are three stones, then the number of possible combinations is six."

"Wouldn't it be three?"

"Try it yourself."

Lien squatted and arranged the stones this way and that, while counting. "You're right. Five, no, six ways."

David found seven more stones and placed them in a pile next to the first three. As he spoke, I translated. "Ten stones yield more than three and a half million possible combinations."

Lien gasped. "That's a lot!" She crouched over the pile, arranging them as if she were a con artist doing three-card monte in Times Square.

The Tamagotchi on her wrist hadn't beeped all day. When I asked her about it, Lien pressed a button and held up the tiny screen for me to see. A pixelated spirit flew in the air above the line that represented the land. "I took good care of it, so my Tamagotchi died naturally. She's now in heaven with Grandma and all the angels and Buddhas!"

I smiled.

Ten fish were not static like stones, and their motion create a multitude of permutations. If those fish were people, with more options and more ambitions, then the permutations, the ways that lives unfolded, were infinite.

Ainara pointed at the stones piled at our feet and said to Lien, "Your grandmother told us each stone was a story." She picked up a pink stone and placed it in my palm. "This stone is the story of you. Take it with you."

I closed my hand.

I wouldn't make the same mistakes with my sister that I'd made with my mother.

We walked back toward the convenience store. I stroked the western wall, scarred from the years and harsh winters. The brick radiated warmth.

A ladybug landed on the back of my hand, and another on my wrist, above my newly formed lightning tattoo.

I lifted my hand to study them. The ladybug on my wrist beat its wings then flew off to land on the wall. The other ladybug joined it.

Ainara said to Lien, "Ladybugs are maps for life. Each of the dots on their bodies are a dream, or a meal, or a laugh, or a loss, like a book you write in all your life."

My sister spoke in my mother's voice, an autumn wind in a warm sunset.

The black dots on the ladybugs glowed white with inner light.

Lien jumped and skipped, chasing the ladybugs as they landed on the wall. "It's hard to read their stories when they won't stop moving," she said.

The ladybugs danced, preferring the old bricks to the new, as if age held more heat and resonance.

I held up my camera and took a photo.

I turned the wheel to advance to the next frame, but it only moved a fraction of a turn. I had reached number thirty-six: the last photo on the roll.

TWENTY-ONE

That evening, I sat again with my father and we drew a calendar, for a year this time instead of a month.

As I inked in the days of the week, I saw that each line, from left to right, was a journey of days into the future, each line from top to bottom a trip of months. Memories are created at the intersection of time and place. When either changed, I changed.

When we were done, I marked on the calendar when we would be back to see them.

I was leaving my home of Eternal Spring and going to my home of New York City. For me, it was not only possible but necessary to have two homes. To be whole, I needed both the place I came from and the place I chose.

When I hugged my aunt Eyun goodbye, I whispered, "I'm sorry you never found love."

She murmured back, "I've always had love. I was looking for someone to share it."

THE AFTERNOON WE got back, David wanted nothing but sleep, and I wanted nothing but wakefulness. When I tucked him into bed, he said, "I love you."

I walked south from our apartment, and I saw America again as if for the first time. Jet lagged, I found the streets of New York City paved with diamonds. Light shone on both sides of the buildings.

At 87th Street, a man came out of a grate in the ground carrying a fifty-pound bag of flour. He whistled at me as I passed.

In Midtown, I stood in the valley of tall buildings. I looked up and counted: *Yi, er, san, si . . . er shi* for twenty, then switched into English, twenty-one, twenty-two, twenty-three . . . Somewhere around sixty-eight, I blinked and lost track of the stories.

I imagined the buildings unzipping, laying bare the people inside, who had even more stories than the buildings did.

The sun set, a sliver of light between cement giants. The plate-glass windows shimmered, buildings facing buildings, mirrors reflecting mirrors, lacy wings in the wind. I could catch the sun's rays on my face if I chased it, dodging people too busy to notice the light.

After sunset, what New York City lacked in daylight and starlight, it made up for in neon, fluorescent and incandescent.

At 51st, while I waited to cross the street, a man who smelled of whiskey called, "Wear a G-string, make fifty dollars!" Fifty dollars was four hundred yuan, or about how much my sister earned in a month. I crossed the street when the light changed. He followed me halfway before returning to his corner.

Twin teenage girls emerged from Sbarro's pizzeria on 47th and skipped down the street, giggling and laughing. The first looked to the sky and shouted, "Marco!"

The other girl yelled, "Polo!"

I wondered why they were shouting the name of a long-dead explorer.

I crossed to the traffic island in the center of Times Square and stopped. I held out my arms to embrace the city, the sky, the world that was new again.

My irises dilated in the light created by Coca-Cola and Sbarro, Suntory liquor and *CATS* the Musical.

To my right, drunken club kids joked in voices so slurred I thought they were speaking another language. To my left, taxis honked. A woman behind me sang "Amazing Grace," and her voice floated up through the lights and echoed between the neon billboards.

Light surrounded the buildings. No shadows.

I filled my lungs with the iron and geranium smell of New York City. I tasted metal in the back of my throat, a lingering open-mouth kiss from the city.

I turned my hands to make a rectangular frame with my thumbs and forefingers. I pointed my hands at tourists strolling arm in arm, at the space between cars as they stopped and started, at the woman singing. Whenever I had a perfect photo within the frame, I closed my hands into fists, as if I could collapse the reality of time and

Times Square into myself and capture those moments forever.

Ten years ago, when I first came to New York, I had done this same walk. Then, I was a child who had moved by herself to a new country in search of a dream, of a photo, of a new life. Now, I was an adult with two countries and a life filled with art and love.

I wandered the streets for half the night, drinking in the sights of New York City with my eyes and my ears and my breath.

When I got back to the apartment, David was still asleep. Not yet ready to go to bed, I stepped into the darkroom and reveled in the metallic chemical taste of the air. The red safelight cast a dim illumination onto the table, the cat's cradle of photos hung on lines, and me. I was grateful to see everything.

It was my first moment alone in many days, but I didn't feel lonely. I carried my family in my memories.

I also carried memories in the disposable camera in my hands. I had to destroy it to develop the photos I'd taken in China. While I knew the camera was nothing but cardboard and plastic, for a moment, I was sad. My father's voice came to me: "It's not the metal and glass and clay that's art. The effect it has on us—that is art."

I turned off the safelight and blinked, more familiar now than ever with darkness. I unrolled and dipped and dunked. The diesel vinegar scent of developing fluid filled my nose.

I realized that in choosing how to light a subject, the angle to shoot at, what to crop out and what to leave in, I changed the story. To write a book is to tell a story; to paint a painting is to tell a story; to take a photo is to tell a story. Every artistic endeavor has the same goal.

The story is only half-formed when I take a photo. The other half is created by the viewer.

I usually printed a thumbnail sheet of all the photos, then picked a few to print as 8 x 10s. This time, I printed every photo large so that I could better see my journey home.

When I emerged from the darkroom, I frowned. While I'd been locked inside, our apartment had rained Post-it Notes.

Yellow slips of paper flew like tiny flags from every object. I peered at the one attached to the darkroom door. On it was David's handwriting in English: Darkroom; Eyun's in Chinese: *Anshi*; and my grandmother's in Manchu.

I read the note on the wall, again written in all three languages. The closet, my alarm clock, the bed. Our apartment full of Post-it Notes, each one naming something three ways.

Through the ocean of yellow paper ran a line of red Post-it Notes, each with a word written on it, only in English. I followed the red ribbon, reading the words out loud. They led me to David in the kitchen, where he was labeling the fridge.

Together, the slips of paper told a story: "I thought I would learn Chinese and you can relearn Manchu." As I read the last word, I thought my heart might explode from joy.

"Aimee," he whispered.

We said to each other sweet nothings and sweet everythings. In this other country, I now had my true name.

I looked at him and felt as I had when we fell in love: alive, emboldened, full of possibilities. David wrote two Chinese words on the Post-it Note in his hand, and handed it to me.

Ai ren.

Beloved.

TWENTY-TWO

When I finally slept, I dreamed of my mother.

We moved an earthenware jar as tall as my shoulder. She lifted one edge, then turned it forward, so that the part of the base that remained on the ground dug in like a harrow. I helped steady the balance. She switched her hands to the opposite edge, then lifted and turned. In this way, she and I "walked" the jar from the root cellar hut to the yard.

"Mother, isn't it unsanitary? The outside of the jar is all nice and glazed so things wash off easily. The inside is earth. You can't ever get it clean."

She smiled and pulled my braid. The lines of branched lightning on her wrist glowed pink. "We're not going to get it clean, Aimee. Clean doesn't taste very good. Your grandmother's magic teapot makes tea without tea leaves for the same reason. This jar drank from the salt and spices of previous years, so all those flavors will help to flavor this year."

Yen's father and my father had lined two rectangular tables side by side to make one square table. Many people toiled around it.

My grandmother washed Chinese cabbage. Yen's mother was cutting cabbage; she had been cutting cabbage forever. She stacked the two-inch-square slices neatly on the table. When the stacks grew tall enough to hide her, they fell over like trees in a mudslide, ending up a jumbled heap.

Yen was crushing dried whole hot peppers. He had tied a handkerchief over his face to guard against inhaling pepper powder. He placed the peppers by the handful into a wooden mortar, then pounded them with a bulbous pestle. Yen's father had carved the mortar and pestle from the root of a linden tree.

My father was cutting Chinese radish into slices. When he finished with the radishes, he set to work clobbering ginger roots with a mallet.

Ainara was peeling garlic. Grandfather Feng was needlessly stirring a bucket of salt.

My mother handed me a knife and eight pears. "Chop each of these into eight pieces." I obeyed, cutting the pears into eight pieces and discarding the seeds. She did the same with eight apples.

Yen's mother's pile of chopped cabbage became a stage curtain. I only knew she was behind there because she was singing in Manchu.

My mother approached her with a bowl and scooped piles of cabbage leaves into it. She joined in the song. She poured the leaves into the bottom of the jar we had moved from the storage shed.

She gestured and Ainara brought the bucket of salt, hugging it to her chest. Ainara didn't know the words to the song but happily hummed the tune.

I had learned the Chinese lyrics in school, but not the Manchu ones. My Mandarin overlapped my mother's Manchu; the song progressed unhindered.

My mother ladled a cup of salt into the jar. My grandmother approached and added radish slices. Humming, almost dancing, Yen's mother added a fistful of red pepper flakes and some ginger. Ainara ran up with her hands full of garlic, dropping the cloves into the jar at my mother's nod.

My mother climbed onto a stool so the lip of the jar was at waist level. As she leaned into the jar, her heels came off the stool. She continued singing, the song distorting and thrumming warmly against the earthen sides. She moved the ingredients inside the jar with her spatula and placed a circle of pears in a layer around the perimeter of the pot.

When she emerged, she sneezed from the pepper. Her voice was more vibrant when she rejoined the singing.

Yen's mother came around with more cabbage leaves, to which we added another layer of salt, pepper flakes, ginger, garlic, pear. Every now and again, my mother sprinkled white pepper into the jar.

When the jar was about a third full, my mother rolled up the hem of my pants until they resembled shorts. She lifted me under my armpits and stood me in a metal trough of water, where she scrubbed me from thighs to toes and back up again with a hog bristle brush. I giggled when the brush reached the soles of my feet. I sang in between giggles.

Everyone paused in their work and watched us.

"Ready?" my mother asked.

"Ready."

My mother lifted me from the trough, held me in midair to drip dry for a moment, then deposited me in the jar. The soles of my feet touched slick cabbage and a clove of garlic lodged between my toes.

"Jump! Jump! Up and down!" Ainara shouted, demonstrating.

"Don't jump up and down," my grandmother said. "If you jump up and down it will form air bubbles in the *La Bai Cai* and ruin it." *La Bai Cai* literally means spicy white vegetables—preserved to keep us alive through winter. "You want to press the air bubbles out without causing any new ones. Step, but slowly."

With my mother holding my left arm to help me keep balance, I lifted my right foot, feeling my weight shift and the left one sink farther into the vegetables. I put my right one down and lifted the left foot. Vegetables and liquid seeped up to my ankle.

I worked up a slow rhythm. After a few moments, my mother let go of my arm and returned to her task of ferrying cabbage. I turned in a circle as I stepped, and she added more ingredients around my legs.

"I bet you want to be me," I called to Ainara.

Ainara pouted and fingered her scabbed left knee. She'd tripped over the door stoop two days earlier while Yen had been chasing her in a game of Catch the Robber.

She said, "I want to jump up and down in the jar!"

My grandmother said, "You can't stand in hot pepper when you have a cut. It will hurt."

"But it looks like so much fun."

I stole bits of cabbage leaves and radish and garlic as my mother added them. Their taste was green and raw and bitter. I dipped my thumb in a passing handful of pepper flakes and tasted it, the heat making my eyes water.

As I stepped, I remembered how the *La Bai Cai* tasted in the middle of winter. I tried to commingle the individual flavors into a medley—a symphony of raw ingredients and the passage of time.

In November the *La Bai Cai* would be crunchy and taste lightly salted, with cloves of garlic occasionally rolling around in my mouth whole. By February the garlic would have melted, the ginger turned into threads of nothing but fiber. The salty and spicy, the sweet and sour, would draw fully into the cabbage by osmosis. As spring drew closer, the preserves tasted more sour, even though we never added any vinegar. Time was what yielded that alchemy of tangy deliciousness.

Once in a while, my chopsticks would reach for a cabbage leaf and pull up a slice of pear. The sweetness of fruit piqued by pepper and ginger was overwhelming, and always put a smile on my face. "Why don't we put more fruit into the jar?" I asked.

My mother said, "That would make the fruit less special. A good thing, when there is too much of it, can be a bad thing."

My legs warmed from the spices: pepper and ginger and garlic helping my circulation as I was helping them to harmonize.

My father and Yen's father moved another jar into the yard. They chanted the part of the song that is spoken and not sung.

I hummed along, then mimed the chorus in Manchu as my mother and Yen's sang.

By the time the first jar was three-quarters full, I had to crouch and hold on to the lip so as not to fall. My cheeks had flushed, both from exertion and from the pepper that had seeped through my skin and into my veins. My toes and ankles tingled, electrified.

My mother lifted me and placed me in the next jar.

We made four jars of *La Bai Cai*, two for us and two for Yen's family. They were to stand guard next to the kitchen door of each house, there to remain and be eaten throughout the coming winter.

When my mother lifted me from the last jar, my lower legs and feet were a cheerful sunset orange, and I had learned to sing the song in Manchu.

TWENTY-THREE

I returned to where it all started.

At the vegetable stall in Chinatown, the old Manchu woman looked up with surprise. "You want vegetable? Or letter read?"

I spoke in Manchu, tasting each word as it left my mouth. "Vegetables. And I came to bring you a part of our homeland."

She frowned and narrowed her eyes. "You speak Manchu now, do you?"

I nodded. "Always did. I just had to remember the words."

Her warm laughter wafted over me, reminding me of Feng. She flung her arms wide and knocked over a stack of peppers. "Did you bring me a rock? Some dirt?" She restacked the peppers into a neat pyramid.

I opened my purse and pulled out an 8 x 10 flat package wrapped in kraft paper. "I didn't know what town you're from, so I brought this from my village."

She rubbed her hands down her denim apron to clean them, then unwrapped my gift.

She frowned and pointed at the center of the photo. "What is this?"

"That's my father's light from the Moon Festival lantern competition. Around it are my family and fellow villagers."

Her finger circled the frame. "And this? How is there a town gate and a mountain and a river in the same photo? Are those ladybugs?"

"When my father's light rotated, it cast shadows onto us of all the elements of Eternal Spring. But a single photo couldn't capture that, so I printed the photos of the village gate, Ice Dragon Mountain and the River of Stories all into one." I had also layered in the last photo I took in China, of my sister and Lien standing before the western wall of our house surrounded by ladybugs.

The vegetable seller pursed her lips and shook her head. "This town gate says Eternal Spring, so this is the Black Dragon Mountain and the Black Dragon River."

"No, the mountain is the Ice Dragon Mountain and the river is the River of Stories, because that is what my mother called them."

She scrutinized me, then brushed her eyelashes with her knuckle and laid the photo on top of a stack of Chinese cabbage. She turned to help a man choosing peppers. I waited until she finished, then bought two bags of vegetables and fruit. As she bagged my purchase, I held up my new digital camera and took a photo of her.

Despite telling myself I didn't need to check the screen right away—I'd lived my whole life without the instant gratification of digital—I looked anyway. The old woman in the photo was lit perfectly, the wrinkles on her knuckles sharp.

I turned the camera to show her the photo on the inch-square display.

She laughed. "Why, that's me. How did you take my photo and make me appear immediately?"

I shrugged and smiled. "It's easy. I'm a shaman."

Her eyes met mine. "This is better than rocks or dirt." She caressed the right edge of the frame, drawing my eyes to the part of the photo that contained Ainara and Lien, holding hands before the western wall of our childhood home in the last photo I took in China. The red brick wall teemed with ladybugs lit flaming orange by the sunset.

I knew then, with the giddy clairvoyance of falling in love: this was the photo.

I traced the blurry right side, and my fingertips tingled with the shock of contact. I leaned in, thinking of my sister, my niece, my mother.

My hand trembled.

Heat surges up my arm until I could taste fire in my mouth.

I fall.

I emerge in Eternal Spring on that autumn day. Lien jumps up and down, chasing the ladybugs that soar and land interminably.

A ladybug settles on the tip of my nose. I cross my eyes to look at it. When I blink, it transfigures. The black dots on its body glow with light.

The sun sets, and countless lights illuminate us.

Lien jumps, Ainara smiles, and standing between them my mother laughs.

The camera I'd lost on my journey home is cradled in my hand. I lift the viewfinder to my eye and take a photo of my mother.

My mother lives.

<<<<>>>>

CREDITS

ANGEL DI ZHANG and Random House Canada would like to thank everyone who worked on the publication of *The Light of Eternal Spring* in Canada.

EDITORIAL
Anne Collins
Deirdre Molina
Lauren Park
Sue Kuruvilla

COPY EDITOR
Tilman Lewis

PROOFREADER
Eleanor Gasparik

DESIGN
Jennifer Griffiths

PRODUCTION
Trina Kehoe
Terra Page
Tristan Dodge

AUDIO
Jaclyn Gruenberger
Caleb Stull

CONTRACTS
Samantha North
Jamie Steep
Naomi Pinn

SALES
Evan Klein

MARKETING
Anais Loewen-Young
Danya Elsayed

PUBLICITY
Chalista Andadari

EDITORIAL ACQUISITION BOARD
Kristin Cochrane
Barry Gallant
Scott Sellers
Marion Garner

ANGEL DI ZHANG was born in northeast China, and raised in China, England, Canada and the United States. She was educated in the joint BA-MIA program at Columbia University, and is a painter and an internationally exhibited fine art photographer. She lives in a secret garden near Toronto.

ACKNOWLEDGMENTS

IT IS MY name on the cover, but I and this book would not be what we are without you. I am sincerely grateful.

My one true editor, Anne Collins: You see me. Your edits are brilliant, and your questions bring out my best. I'm thrilled by the entire process of making this book with you.

My champion, Jon Michael Darga: I am glad every day that you are my friend and agent. Your kindness, humanity and editing genius inspire me.

My best friend and first reader, Merav Hoffman: You have been with me since the first chapter. You are the wind beneath my wings.

Thank you, friends who read early versions of this manuscript and offered thoughts, critique and encouragement. Eugene Myers, Deborah J. Brannon, Michael W. MacNeil, Irene Katzela, Jack Fischer, Priya Mathur, Francisco Calisto Richter, Sze K. Chan, Alexander, Julie Ayotte, Barry Wallace and Lani Frank.

Thank you, Rebecca Faith Heyman, and your brilliant brainchild, The Work Conference. Wayson Choy, Susan Breen and my muse Paula Munier. My mentor Michelle Hauck, Brenda Drake and all my siblings in Pitch Wars 2019.

The Fork Family: You make this writing life a joy. I am a child of many places but among you I belong and am home.

My ADZ grant committee: Sami Ellis, Kate Dylan, Sarah Rana Mughal, Gigi Griffis, Chandra Fisher, A. Y. Chao, Amanda Helander, Emily Varga and Molly Steen. We are going to change the world for the better.

My gratitude to the Canada Council for the Arts and the Ontario Arts Council. Your grants gave me the gift of time, and all I can do is repay that with art.

My parents: Thank you for giving me life, love and an education.

My grandmother, aunts and uncles: Thank you for everything in my childhood and now.

The love of my life and the love of my every lifetime, Alexander: Your faith in me makes it possible for all my dreams to come true.